Melisha Ross

PRINTHOUSE BOOKS
PRESENTS

I0609977

Ionia
The beginning of the End
Paranormal Fiction

MELISHA ROSS

Ionia

©MELISHA ROSS; 2014

PrintHouse Books, Atlanta, GA.
Published 12 -20 -2014
www.PrintHouseBooks.com

**VIP INK Publishing Group;
Incorporated**

Cover art, designed by SK7.
Editor: Che' Y Middlebrooks
ISBN: 978-1-63102-995-0

Library of Congress Cataloging-in-Publication Data

MELISHA ROSS

Ionia: *The beginning of the End*

1. Paranormal 2.Fiction 3.Sci-fi
4.Urban Literature
5. MELISHA ROSS

Ionia

In a world filled with lies, infidelity and pain it is hard to see the positive things that surround us because we cannot see through the clouds of negativity, which overshadow our lives. Right in the heart of Grand Rapids Michigan a family finds themselves fighting to preserve all that is good and familiar, while battling against the unknown. Little do they know that beyond the surface is a world that few can imagine exists. Kenny and Samantha are about to find out that all the things they were told as a child, the ghost stories of those that walk amongst us, are not really stories at all.

It will take a special innocents to see past, what is on the other side, they will be tested physically and mentally but the gift of one child will be the difference of force to help them see. Kenny, Samantha and their

4

son Keyvon are on a ride for their lives; yet the future of millions rest on the shoulders of one little girl, who doesn't even know it yet.

Come take this journey down the beaten path with ionia.

I dedicate this book to those whom have ever lost someone special. For myself I remember my Dad Earl Hall, Grandmother Lurenda Hall, my friends Angela Hardy and Troy. Our souls live on as well as the love felt which will never die. I also dedicate this book to my mother Zelmar Hall and my brothers Jermaine, Earl, and Michael Hall. To my Grandmother Maggie Hollis, my many aunts, uncles, cousins and friends; I say thank you for your love and support. To my two children, Mckalen and Angelic, Mommy loves you very much and always will.

MELISHA ROSS

Ionia
The beginning of the End
Paranormal Fiction

**VIP INK Publishing Group,
Incorporated**
Atlanta, GA

Ionia

Table of Contents

Chapter 1
In the Beginning

Nestled in a grand city, on the corner of Watkins and Dallas Street; stood a two story, grey house with a porch the size of its entirety. This home although 30 plus years old; was still by far the most beautiful on its block.

The neighborhood however, was not the everyday garden variety; you could tell that at one point in time, was a remarkable place to live. Cement sidewalks with multiple cracks, grass the darker shade of brown and filth from trash; from careless passer byres filled the streets and worse still violence covered the surrounding areas; making it unbearable to raise children.

The people who lived in this neighborhood have resided there for many years; they have seen good times as well as bad times, weddings, funerals, births and more. Everyone knew each other and took care of one other, because they knew that it took a village to raise a child; which in the year of 2011 was very rare to find.

This is Michigan, the home of Motown, General Motors, and the famous Kellogg's Cereal.

The Murphy's reside in this home; they were somewhat new to the area, not many people knew very much about them. Kenny the head of the household relocated his family from Fort Bragg, after retiring from the military due to injuries sustained in the Iraq war.

It was a close call to death for Kenny; the doctors did not believe that he would make it, and if by chance he did, they thought he would never walk again.

Kenny beat the odds, with only scars left to his abdomen; but his wounds went further than his scars, he loved the military life; it was all he knew and even though he was discharged honorably, emotionally he was let down.

Kenny's parents had died suddenly when he was thirteen years old due to a tragic accident, when his parents were killed in a house fire while vacationing in Colorado; many believed that Kenny's life had been saved because he was attending a summer camp while they were away.

Foster home to foster home was his life until he graduated high school and found solace in the Army. Aside from his wife Samantha or Sam for short and his son Keyvon the military was all that he had in his life.

Even though life has thrown him a monkey wrench at each turn emotionally, physically you could not tell; he carried himself very well, the ladies seemed to drop to his feet without him uttering a word. No woman could resist his chocolate smooth skin; light colored eyes, baldhead and smile, which were bright enough to melt the hardest heart.

All of those women however could not compare to Sam, she was the one that almost got away in his eyes. Sam wasn't impressed by his physical appearance, she became his best friend.

Samantha was not a ugly women by all means, a beauty to all that glanced in her direction from the black hair that flowed like a river to her waist line, green eyes, high cheek bones and body built like a Amazon queen. If there really were a Venus goddess of love, she would be one

Jealous woman while in the presents of Sam. Samantha was not new to the military life as a matter of fact, her father retired after 22 years of service in the army. It was by chance the two had met; she was running an errand for her father at the commissary, when she ran into Kenny and an instant conversation struck.

Five years and one child later the two are still together. The road within their marriage has been a rough one but they believed that it was worth the fight. They felt as if they were back on the right track; with their son Keyvon now two years old, they are glad for their relocation away from everything that was familiar.

Kenny smiles at how far they had come; things were going in the right direction, or so he thought.

Samantha pulls into the driveway reaches for the sun visor, so that she can click the button on the garage door opener. It's raining outside, puddles of water overflowing with every raindrop; she can't help but become a bit pissed, thinking of the amount of money that she spent getting her hair done for this date.

The engine comes to a halt after she turns the key to park the car in the port. Damn! I sure hope that he is still sleeping. The clock revealing the time of 3:00 in the morning as she starts to kick around in her head where she had been if he was up waiting, she needed the perfect lie to cover up.

For all Kenny knew she was at dinner with her friend celebrating a birthday, she couldn't believe how very gullible her husband had become over the years.

With purse in hand she reaches to the back seat of her Mitsubishi Eclipse, grabs her coat, steps out of the car and heads towards the back door. The sound of rain drops taping against nearby tree leaves are mixed with the sounds of mud being stepped on.

Shoot my shoes! Sam bends downward to check out the damage made to her black leather 3-inch stilettos. The back door is within arm's reach; as she pauses to fumble for the key she looks up to the bedroom window to make sure there is no inkling of movement.

Good no lights! The master bedroom window faced the backyard so it was easy enough for her to tell if anyone was there; unlike tonight's stormy night you could see the stars in the sky, and during the day you could see all the way into the room of the house directly behind it, if you wanted to be a nosey neighbor.

There is not just one door but two that she has to go through to gain entrance to the house; they had placed a light screen door in front of the main door, so when it was summer they could leave the oak door open to circulate air through the house.

The screen door was the hardest to master because one quick

move would snap the door back and it's sound could be heard all through the house like the crack of a whip. On the other hand if the door was closed too slowly you could hear the metal creaking like nails to a chalkboard.

Click! The sound of the key turning to open the screen door to Sam was in comparison to a horn being blown to wake up a group of cadets in the morning.

Holding the screen door open, she takes the same key and unlocks the oak door behind it; walks through and simultaneously closes the screen door.

Most mid west homes were made with basements, so when you walk in the back door you have the option to go down a flight of stairs to the basement or up 3 stairs to walk into the middle of the home. Sam with a sigh a relief opens the last door that leads into their kitchen.

Pain is shooting up her legs from wearing her heels all night long, so she takes them off places them at the door, walks into the dining room and gently puts her purse on the table.

A light blinks on and off; she catches the glow from her peripheral vision. Okay now I am seeing things. The light flickers again. I know that there were no lights on when I got in here.

A sudden uneasiness comes over her as she starts to walk into the living room where she saw this light; she wasn't sure if it was the small bit of guilt that was bothering her or if she really felt like someone was watching her.

A puzzled look comes over her face as she feels her way around the dining room table and peeks her head into the living room, realizing that there is no one there; she starts to feel as if she is losing her mind so she turns around, walks back through the door and begins up the stairs to second level where the rooms are located.

Samantha finally gets all of her clothes off and gently slides in the bed behind Kenny with her back facing him, and then she closes her eyes. Kenny feels the motion from the bed opens his eyes and glances at the clock. 3:15. She is at her shit again! I'll drill her about it in the morning.

Time 5:00 am

Kenny, with a sudden yell, jolts his body straight up; sweat dripping profusely against his brow. Get down! We are under attack! Samantha startled out of her sleep in fear of her life.

What's going on? Sam looks over to her husband; seeing his eyes are still close and body shaking; Kenny! Kenny! Sam shakes him. Wake up it's just a dream. Not a surprise to Sam at all, that this has happened she has dealt with it for some time now; she had grown a little agitated by his Post Traumatic Stress Disorder, so she turns over and wraps herself back under the covers and falls back to sleep.

Kenny opens his eyes after being shaken by his wife to hear her cold condescending voice; he watched as she turns over to resume her sleeping. Kenny is amazed at how uncaring she has become, hurt that she didn't even try to make sure he was okay, he starts to become anger and says to himself; Bitch!

Kenny grabs a hold of his side of the covers rolls over and tries to muster up the last piece of pride he has left. Sorry for waking you Sam. In return there was silence in the air.

Morning has arrived in the Murphy home. You can see the early morning rays shimmering through the shades of the window, which were cracked, open just enough to create vertical lines on the adjacent wall.

The alarm clock on the dresser on Kenny's side of the bed sounds. Kenny buried deep under the red plush comforter reaches one arm out hastily to find the snooze button to shut it off.

The covers slowly start to peel away and like a submarine his body starts to emerge from under. 8:00 a.m.; Kenny slowly starts to inch out of their beautiful white oak king size bed, trying carefully not to wake up his wife.

Ring, Ring! Startled In the middle of stretching Ken rushes over to his cell phone still lying on the top of the dresser plugged up to its charger. Hello? Kenny lowers his voice a little, looks over to his wife still lying in bed, making sure she is still asleep. Slipping on his slippers place at the foot of the bed on the floor he walks quietly into the bathroom and closes the door behind him.

Sam opens up one eye and listens as the door closes to the bathroom, then sits up in disgust.

Curiosity is growing thicker in her mind so she decides to quickly slide off her side of the bed and tip toe to the door to take a listen in on his conversation.

I was just about to call you. No, no you didn't wake me. Sam? Oh yeah she is still sleep. No, I cannot meet with you on Wednesday; Friday is actually better, that way Sam will be at work.

I will just drop my son off early to daycare, that way we will have enough time with no interruptions. Samantha's curiosity has now turned into anger. Okay, well I will give you a call a little later with the details; you know time and place things of that matter.

Sam realizes that Ken is about to end the conversation and darts back across the room, jumps into bed and pulls the covers over her body. Okay Tonya talk to you soon. Kenny ends the call and opens up the door. He sees movement from under the covers but chalks it up to her just moving about trying to get comfortable.

Sam's rage coupled with her rapid breathing is now creating nothing but heat that is now becoming too hard to bear.

Kenny finds a spot on the bed next to Sam and sits beside her. He places his hand gently on her leg caresses her. Sam, Sam. Sweetie would you like some breakfast? Sam jerks her leg from under his touch, and makes a moaning noise.

Sam peeks from under the cover at Kenny. Oh! I am sorry Ken, yes please; I will wake up Keyvon in a minute. Kenny nods his head in agreement. I will let you guys know when it's done.   Kenny leans over and gives Samantha a kiss on her forehead, stands up, puts his robe on and walks out the room to the kitchen.

Samantha watches Kenny as he walks out of the room. I cannot believe the nerve of him putting his lips on me, after those same lips whispered sweet nothings to another woman! Maybe he needs to save them for his little mistress.

Sam rubs her forehead as if she was taking off the print from his kiss, grabs her robe, walks to the bathroom and starts to run her some bath water. I don't even know why I even stay. Slam! The door shuts.

You can hear the sounds of pots clanging while they are being brought out of the cabinets and plates clicking against the kitchen table, as they are being set by

Ionia

Kenny   downstairs   preparing
breakfast.

The smell of turkey bacon, eggs,
biscuits,   coffee   and   freshly
squeezed orange juice lingered in
the air. Keyvon who was still
asleep upstairs in his room smells
the aroma of the food being
prepared opens his eyes and
takes in a long sniff.

Slowly pulling back his covers,
which   were   decorated   with
spider man, his favorite hero; he
swings his legs over the edge of
the bed and plants his feet on the
floor. Mommy!

Keyvon pauses a moment, he
doesn't hear his mother answer
so he stands up and walks across
the hallway to his parent's door
and knocks lightly.

Sam just finishing up her bath
and drying off puts the rest of her

clothes on. Come in! Hi baby did you sleep well last night? No, mommy I had a really bad dream. Awe sweetie I am sorry, tell me about it.

Samantha lays down her rob across the bed, grabs a hold of Keyvon's hand, walks him over to the bed and sits him on the edge. Sam sits beside him. Tell me about it sweetie.

Well, there was this really mean monster that was chasing me, he said he was going to come and get me real soon. Disbelief crosses over Sam's face as her mouth drops open.

Keyvon sweetie, it is all only a dream; no one is coming to get you, besides you have me and daddy to protect you. Bam! A sound of glass cracking and a small thud makes Sam and

Keyvon body jolts up from being startled.

What was that mommy? Sam glances in the direction the noise came from and peeks at the floor. Man! Samantha gets up off the bed and reaches down on the floor.

Oh, sweetie the picture just fell off the dresser; I will put another one up, it is okay. Go ahead and wash your face and hands so we can go downstairs and eat breakfast. Okay, mommy.

Keyvon runs into the bathroom and runs the water to the sink. I will be there in a sec to help you Keyvon. Sam picks up the picture frame that she had handcrafted at a local frame shop on Eastern and Burton St.

She smiles picking up the picture while remembering more happy days with her husband.

Sam can't help but to wonder however; how the frame could have fell, it was sitting far away from the edge of the dresser, closer to the mirror; the frame is connected with screws so that it doesn't move.

Looking closely at the picture of Keyvon when he had turned 1 year old, she notices what seemed like a smudge on the face; she peels off the lingering glass from the edges and takes a closer look. That's no smudge! Sam takes the picture out and looks closely once more. Oh my God how could that have happened!

Keyvon's face was instead clear, as a bell is now blurry and distorted. Sam shrugs it off, places the fragments of glass in the trash, vacuums up the smaller pieces and goes into the bathroom and helps Keyvon with his face and hands.

Hey guys' breakfast is ready! The Two of them hear Kenny yelling for them to come downstairs to eat. We will be there in a minute Ken. Sam gets the towel from the cabinet, dries his face and hands. Come on lets go eat breakfast with daddy.

Kenny places the last bit of food on the plates arranged on the table. He hears light footsteps walking in front and the heavier in the back along the hallway floors upstairs, letting him know they were on their way downstairs.

The footsteps abruptly stop at the top of the stairs, followed by a slam coming from one of the room doors. Heavier foots steps followed them moving down the hallway.

Keyvon go down stairs to daddy! Kenny hears this whisper coming from Sam.
His little feet could be heard running down the stairs. Daddy! Mommy can't move! She is stuck! Kenny bends the corner to reach the bottom of the stairs and is greeted with a scared little two year old.

Kenny picks him up and glances to the top of the stairs and sees Sam standing there as if in a trance. Sam! Sam! She doesn't move, so he raises his voice a little more and puts more tone to it. Sam! The trance that had taken a hold over her seemed to have had dissipated. Kenny, did you see that? See what Sam? It was standing right there Ken. Sam points in the direction she was staring in.

Kenny starts to make his way up the flight of stairs slowly, while taking short looks up and over the banister to see if he could get a glimpse of what she is talking about; but when he reaches the top nothing is there.

Keyvon's little body is shaking in fear, so Kenny places him in his mother's arms and starts to walk slowly down the hallway bracing himself for anything that may jump out at him. Kenny walks into his
son's room first, looking under the bed, in the closet and checking the windows. All clear in here babe!

Kenny then crosses the hallway into their room checks and checks their and hers walk in closet, under the bed, in the bathroom and again checking the window.

On the way back out of the room he sees the picture of Keyvon laying on the dresser with the frame broken in two; he then notices the face blurred out.

Humph! I wonder how that could have happened. Kenny shakes his head and places the picture back down. I'll ask her what happened later on.

Closing the bedroom door behind him he starts walking back toward Sam and his son. What exactly did you see, there is no one here? Kenny it was a dark mass with glowing red eyes; it didn't have any legs it was just hovering there staring at me, it even growled at me; it said your mine in a very horrific tone. As soon as you came up Ken it disappeared into the wall.

Well, I don't know Sam there is nothing there; it could have been the wind coming through the window that made the door slam shut. What about the dark mist and heavy footsteps then Ken. Sam, it might have been the light from the window casting what may have resembled a shadow on the wall.

Ken, it spoke to me though.
Ken interrupts her because he sees that she is becoming frantic. Let's just go down stairs and have some breakfast before it gets cold.

The three of them make their way downstairs as Ken glances back down the hall way; he feels like something isn't right but he isn't going to let it bother him and further more he didn't want to worry his son.

CHAPTER 2
The Liars We've Become

Utter silence has filled the air; other than the sound of silverware clicking on and off of the plates from the three of them eating at the table, if a pin would have dropped on the floor it would have sounded like a nuclear bomb had just made contact.

So how was your evening with the girls Sam? Sam puts her fork down and clears her throat trying to prevent herself from choking on her food but also the lie she is about to tell. It was good; we just sat around at the restaurant eating and talking is all.

Really! That sounds interesting; so what time did you end up getting in last night Sam? Sam clears her throat once more before speaking

I reached home about 12:30 this morning; I would have gotten here sooner had it not been for it raining so hard on the way home last night, I had to pull over to a rest area on I96 on the way back from Muskegon until it stopped raining. Wow that is something Sam!

That's crazy because I didn't see you here when I came down stairs to get Keyvon a glass of water; he woke up about 1:00 am because he had a bad dream and he was crying. Oh, yeah I crashed on the couch didn't want to wake you up; the lightning got really bad about 3:15am so I went ahead and came up stairs and got in bed.

Kenny starts to clench his jaws tightly because he knows that she is lying to him; he just didn't want to continue because Keyvon was sitting there listening and looking with sad eyes. Don't fight again mommy and daddy! Kenny grabs a hold of his son's hand and reassures him. Oh Key we aren't fighting again we are just talking is all.

Kenny turns in Sam's direction. I am glad that you had a good time with the ladies sweetie; oh by the way I forgot to tell you, on Friday I have to drop Key off a little earlier than usual at daycare; I have a all day meeting to attend and I was wondering can you pick him up for me.

Really what kind of meeting Ken? I have been interested in buying up a couple of duplexes, fix them up and rent them out for some extra income. Wow ken that sounds like a good investment but when were you going to clue me in on it? I just did Sam!

You must excuse my attitude about it all Ken I am just thrown back because this is the first I have heard of this; and where did you get the money to go on this venture? Well it is not set in stone yet Sam; I just want to talk to some investors first and see where it goes; oh, the money is coming from a savings that I had set up a while ago, it takes 20% of my retirement money and moves it over there; don't worry it will not come out of any of our savings. So Ken when where you going to tell me about this separate savings; why would you need a second account?

To be blunt Sam, I was saving it for what do they usually call it a nest egg. Be honest with yourself and us about a year ago given the circumstances did it really seem like we would make it this far?

Sam rolls her eyes and sucks her teeth, whisks the plate off of the table and places the dish in the washer then proceeds to Pull her robe together and tighten it together. Whatever Ken! Then she exits the room.

The sneaky truth is just beneath

8:00 am Friday July, 2011

The sound of water running from the showerhead comes to a halt as the steam from the hot air clouds the bathroom mirror. Sam grabs the towel from its rack located on the wall right next to the shower. Feeling refreshed she steps out from the gliding doors with the towel wrapped around her.

Sam walks over to the sink and reaches under to get her toothpaste tube grabs her tooth brush and goes to whip off the mirror so that she could see, but is stopped when she see a message written on it.

Deceit is just the beginning.

Gasping for breath she covers her mouth in awe. She didn't hear Ken come in the bathroom, does he know of what she is doing? He can't know; I have been careful! All kind of questions are running through her mind at this point.

Kenny! Kenny! Sam opens up the door with attitude. Kenny still sleep in the bed, hearing his wife shouting sits straight up in the bed. What? What? What is wrong; who's there? Did you do this to the mirror Ken? Do what Sam; are you insane? I have been in the bed sleep.

Kenny draws back the covers, pissed off because he was awaken from the middle of his sleep to be accused of something he didn't know about. Ken rushes over to the bathroom and sees the message on the mirror. I didn't write that! Stop playing games it is too early in the morning to start with this Sam.

Whatever Ken, move out of the way please, some of us have to go to work today. Well then go to work then my dear! Kenny turns and walks back towards the bed and climbs back in. I have about another half an hour before I start my day; oh and I love you too Sam. Sam in return slams the door, finishes getting dressed and leaves out to go to work.

Sam reaches work about thirty minutes later. She loves her job; working for the corporate offices of Sage a water brand that was released about two years ago to her was a great opportunity.

With her brown leather brief case in hand she walks in

through the double doors of her building, up the elevator to the 3rd floor and into her office. Still a little shuffled in the head about the conversation that her husband had on the phone with this secret woman, she remembered that he was meeting up with her today.

Sam sits down at her desk and puts her head down into the palms of her hands. Hey Sam! Tameka hey girl, come in. Tameka was the jealous type never positive always managed to bring down any happiness that someone else had. Tameka was so good at it that her victim never knew what was coming till it slapped them in the face.

Tameka was a slender woman around 5′5 in height and about 120 pounds, cute face but her attitude always made any eligible man run in the opposite direction. Sam, why are you looking so glum? It's nothing T. Okay, I know you, something is bothering you and I am not leaving until you tell me what is going on.

Sam takes in a long breath and lifts her head up. I think Ken is seeing someone. Okay Sam, truth being told, you are sleeping around on him. That is not the point T, and I am not sleeping around on him; I have my reasons for doing so. What reasons are those?

He is not the same, I know that he loves me but I still believe that he is still sleeping around; he has no spontaneity for life anymore, the war really, really changed him.

T, he is supposed to be meeting up with her today after he drops off Key. Ooh Sam, I have an idea. What's up T? I say we go and park at the daycare and wait until he comes out and follow him; all of our paper work for inventory is done anyway we are just hanging around here doing nothing, we can slip out and come back without anyone knowing. T, that is a great idea let's go! Sam grabs her keys and purse from off of her desk. I'll drive Sam; he doesn't need to see your car sitting there.

Meanwhile:

The sound of children's laughter filled the hall way to the daycare. Smiling faces fill the rooms eager to teach the young minds sitting in circles. ABCs and 123 songs are being chanted in unison as Kenny and Keyvon walk past the room filled with 4 and 5 year old pre k children.

I want to be in that room daddy! Keyvon waves to the teacher sitting in the middle of the circle, she catches a glimpse of him and waves back at the two of them as they pass by. Soon son you are all most there just 2 more years and you will be there.

The two reach the door of Keyvon's class; with the name of Janice Mackintosh as the lead teach. Mrs. Mackintosh was an older lady around the age of 60 years. It's no surprise that most people could not guess her age she would always have to tell them.

Never in a million years would anyone have a clue that she was that much older because of the way she kept up so well with the children. Hello Mrs. Mackintosh! Kenny smiles as she lifts her head up to greet him. Now I told you about that Ken, it's simply Janice to you. I know but it is a sign of respect Janice, I am truly sorry. Never you mind that. Hi Mrs. Mackintosh!

Keyvon's face lights up with joy as he runs over to her and gives her a big hug. I know I'm a little earlier than usually dropping him off but I have some important business to take care of; Sam will be picking him up this afternoon.

How is she doing? Oh she is okay, thanks for asking. Janice sees the sadness in his eyes and smiles. It's none of my business but I just wanted to say that though you go through hard times and it seems like there is no light at the end of the tunnel, it all works out in the end; at times it may not be what we expected but it was always be meant to be.

Janice has always been a wonderful person to talk to. To Ken she was like the Grandmother that he never got the chance to know. Though she was petite with salt and pepper hair, she had a heart of gold.

Janice's husband had died a few years back; they had been married for 40 years.

To Janice, the children were her comfort; she looked forward to being with them every day. Key was her favorite, she always says that his smile lights up the room and his heart is truly pure. The saying that she used in reference to him was that he was a new soul.

Janice thanks for the words, I wish I could stay and chat with you longer but I have to make this appointment, I will tell you a little more about it later. Okay Ken, it's okay it is story time for the children anyway; we'll talk again sometime soon.

Ken reaches down and gives Key a kiss on his cheek. I will see you later son, be good for Mrs. Mackintosh. Okay daddy I will. I love you! I love you too sport.

Ken waves one last time, exits the room, signs him in and jumps into his 2012 black 4 door Camry.

Meanwhile:

Sam and T slouched down in the car spots Ken getting in the car. There he goes T, he is leaving. The two ladies sit up straight and Tameka starts up the car. Don't get too close T we don't want him to see us. I wonder where he is going! The two follow in pursuit until they come to a star bucks located on the northeast side of the city.

Rage has now set in Sam's hearts as the two ladies watch Ken park the car and walk up to a women sitting at a table placed outside the window with only two chairs.

They park the car on the opposite side of the street and watch through the window.

Omg, Sam I think that you may be right. The two watches as he gives this new lady a hug, kisses her on the cheek and pulls her chair out for her to sit back down.

The lady sits and crosses her legs and flips her hair with a smile as she nods her hair in agreement to whatever they are saying. Sam is fed up at this point. I am ready to go I have seen enough already T. Why don't you go up to them and see what is going on. And what would be my explanation for me being here T; exactly!

Let's go we need to head back anyway I will deal with this in another way. T starts the car and pulls off to head back to work.

Tonya thank you for meeting up with me, I tried to find a half waypoint for the both of us. It's no problem Mr. Murphy; this is actually perfect for me because once I leave this meeting with you I can meet my other client about 10 minutes away.

I want this to be a surprise for Sam, five years together; it's been a long road but we are still together. This is going to be the best anniversary yet. Tonya was a clean cut professional with skin as smooth as a baby's bottom. Her red hair was dark as a ruby without a shimmer of light shining through it.

Very attractive in all essence but not because of her physical beauty but by the confidence that poured out of her pores and drive to be success full. Tonya is no stranger to love she has been married to her husband Richard for the past 10 years and knows all about the ins and outs on how to make a marriage work.

Kenny had come to her knowing her reputation, he had heard about her strong since of style and being able to hone in on what a woman truly wants.

Tonya I want to have the event at the Crown Plaza hotel, in one of the reception halls; I went down there and took a look for myself, it's beautiful and well lit. Have you thought of a color scheme yet Ken?

Well Tonya, not exactly. What is her favorite color? Sam loves the color purple, not just any purple but royal. Ken that is a lovely color! How about a hint of cream, the chairs and the tables can be draped with them? That sounds great! I also need a limousine for that night as well and a room at the Crown as well.

Consider it done Ken. Money is no object. Tonya pulls out her briefcase and starts to show Ken some samples of fabric and colors. For about another hour the two discuss more details. We will make the date for November 3rd. Sounds great Ken that will give us enough time to get everything set up.

Okay I will give you a call to set up another appointment with you okay? Sure that's good let me know Ken. Tonya places her magazines and fabrics back into her briefcase; the two of them shake hands and part their separate ways.

Ken makes his way back to his car parked in the 3rd row of the parking lot. He puts the key into the ignition and crosses over with his right hand and pulls the seatbelt across his chest. Click!

He goes to look through his rear view mirror and notices that it is facing downward.   Hmmph! How did that get moved? He takes his hand and cuffs the top and bottom of the mirror and goes to adjust it properly.

When he moves it up he sees a black mass with red eyes staring back at him. Ahh! Scared out of his wits he quickly turns his head to check the backseat. Nothing is there. Quickly without hesitation he grabs the keys and jumps out of the car. Shit! Shit! Oh my God!

Ken puts his hand over his chest as if to stop his heart from beating too fast. He peers into the back seat looking through the window to make sure nothing is there. Panting rapidly Ken bends forward and cradling his hands on his knees. Man!

I have got to get more sleep; I am starting to see things. Ken starts to laugh at himself. People would think I am crazy. Still a nervous wreck he climbs back into the car and drives down Market St.

This side of town was always a little more peaceful. The main street was made with small reddish bricks pieced together to form a road, though a little bumpy it was kind of soothing to him.

Ken reaches over to the stereo and turns the station to 113.33 FM classic jazz station. With the sounds of Kenny G playing over the speakers, he finds a way to relax. I really need to just calm down. He starts to shake his head and laugh to his self. I must be losing my mind; oh that's right I need to head out to David's bridal so I can pick out Sam's dress.

Kenny cuts off the air conditioner, rolls down the window, puts his shades and heads south towards 28th street.

Back at the office:

Sam tosses her keys on her desk while stumping her feet as she enters her office. I am so pissed right now Tam! Sam calm down lady, everything is going to be okay. I haven't given him any reason to cheat on me; aside from the fact that I am cheating but he doesn't know that I am cheating.

Get real Sam you have a fine specimen of a husband; what woman wouldn't want him. Tam clears her throat before speaking again. Girl except me of course! Have you been satisfying your man; I'm not just talking mentally but also sexually.

Tam that is not yours or anyone else's business how I take care of my man.   I am just saying Sam is giving it up to this guy you are dating...?   Well, I haven't in a while; I just haven't been in the mood.

Well Sam, from the looks of things he is definitely in the mood.   We will talk about this later Tam here comes Tom. I will talk to you later then I have to go and finish up some paper work. Sam pulls up the software to her computer and begins typing away. I'll fix him, for sneaking around on me.

Tap, Tap, Tap! It's not really a nervous rapping of the pencil she is holding but one of anger and plotting. A bright and clever idea pops into her thoughts as if a light bulb had just been screwed on.

Sam reaches for her cell phone in her purse sitting in an empty file cabinet; she keeps her purse there just in case she has to leave the office for a quick moment and wants to not have to take it with her.

Hello Darrius! Yeah it's me Sam; I am at work right now, would you like to meet up for lunch? Okay sounds great. Meet me at Vitale's make it around 1. See you there. Sam ends the call with a slight smirk on her face. Revenge is so sweet.

Sam reaches back down to return her phone to her purse and as she is looking up she hears what sounds like metal slowly screeching. Cautiously she peeks up over her desk and sees the office chair directly in front of her desk is slowly moving up as if someone was adjusting it to take a seat.

Sweat starts to trace the top of her brow as she peers out to the window that is directly behind the chair, but no one but her is seeing this. Thump! The chair then pushes down as if someone has taken a seat and then goes flying across the room hitting the adjacent wall closest to the door.

Oh Shit! Samantha dives back under her desk afraid to dart to the door because the chair is still sitting there. Tears start to swell in her eyes as she tries to figure out how on earth she is going to get out of her office. The office phone rings but she doesn't answer.

Ring! Ring! Samantha sits still in silence with her heart rate climaxing to the point where she was finding it hard to breathe. Ring! Ring! Her cell phone in her purse rings. Samantha scrambles to open the file cabinet door and reaches into her purse and grabs the phone and with a whisper answers. Hello?

Sam, I was trying to call you on the office phone, where are you girl? Tam please come here I am in the office. Sam why are you whispering? Just come here Tam! I'll be there in a minute.

Knock, Knock! Come in! Tam twists the knob to the door and swings open the door to find Sam still nestled under her desk. Girl, why are you under your desk? Tam you wouldn't believe me if I told you, hell I don't even believe what just happened. Well, try me Sam because whatever it is must be serious enough to have a grown woman on the floor.

Sam, plants one foot on the floor firmly and then another, while grabbing the edge of her desk to pull herself up. Tam goes across the room and grabs the chair from the wall and wheels it over to the desk and takes a seat; while Sam takes a seat in her chair. Samantha gathers her thoughts and takes a long deep breath. Don't you laugh Tam because this is serious; you may not believe me but this is what happened.

Sam starts to explain to Tam what happened with the chair in great detail as Tam sits there in disbelief. And that is what happened, Tam. Tam takes a minute to let the situation digest. That is some freaky stuff Sam! Maybe one of the screws on the chair is loose or a wheel is off balance.

Tam gets up out of the chair and starts to investigate. No everything okay there. Tam sighs and puts her hands on her hips with her eyebrows arched;

indicating that she is in deep thought. I don't know Sam, not sure what could have happened.

It's almost lunchtime Sam maybe you need to get some fresh air; I know it could probably be stress especially after this morning's issues. You may be right Sam, I am going to call up Darrius and have him meet me a little earlier. Tam shakes her head in wonder at Sam. She doesn't know what she has at home. Tam, smiles at Sam as she breaks away from her thoughts.

Kenny pulls into the parking lot of Daniel's Bridal boutique located on the south east side of Grand Rapids on 44th street. The ignition to his Navigator comes to a halt as grabs his wallet from the glove compartment, steps out of the car and hits the automatic lock on his key chain.

Ionia

Three women are standing at the front of the store, one at the cash register and the other two are standing at the counter talking. One of the ladies takes a glance out toward the door noticing a glare from the sunlight hitting the glass window.

A smile crosses her face as she turns to the lady standing right next to her and points in Ken's direction.

The third lady that is standing at the cash register; turns her head around as well, then quickly turns back to look at her mirror in haste trying to fix her hair.

Kenny picks up his head from fiddling with his key chain and notices the ladies taking a long look at him. A grin forms but he holds back the laughter so he pushes his chest out a little more and places his shades over his eyes.

The double glass swings open while ken steps in. Hello ladies! Hello Sr.! My name is Tricia, how can I help you? Tricia reminded ken of a young version of Brook Shields, with her long wavy brunette hair, full lips, and hourglass figure.

He starts to feel a bit smitten that this woman who had to be in her late twenties would even look in his direction. Hi Tricia, I am looking for a dress, not for me of course but for my wife. Tricia's face turns into disappointment. Sure Sr. I can help you with that. Do you have a color in mind? Yes Tricia purple, something purple would be great. Oh and please call me Ken. Oh, okay ken; right this way. So what kind of occasion are you celebrating if you don't mind me asking? I am trying to throw a surprise anniversary party.

Awe that is so sweet, well she is a very lucky woman then. Well when you see her Tricia, you make sure to remind her of that. The two start to laugh as they walk to the back of the store to take a look at the various selections.

Do you know her size? Well, not off hand but you look around the same size as her; do you mind trying on a couple of things for me? Well Ken, I would have to ask my manager if it would be okay. Okay and if I need to explain why I will.

Tricia places the 3 dresses that he had pick out on the rack close to the fitting room. I will be right back ken. Ken sits down on the chair seated directly across the fitting room as he waits for her to return. He can't stop thinking about how amazingly beautiful Tricia is and how kind she has been to him just in the last 30 minutes that he had been there. For him the last 30 minutes has been like heaven compared to the last couple of years he has shared with his wife.

Ken! After explaining to my manager the situation she let me know that it would be okay. Great, thank you so much. My pleasure Ken! Tricia picks up the dresses and head into the dressing room.

The curtain opens up and she steps out wearing the first dress. It is a beautiful elegant gown; Sequence from the hem of dress all the way up one side fanning across the bust, which was strapless.

The bust fit perfectly not too loose and not to tight just enough to look like a lady, while the inner lining was white.

You look beautiful; I mean the gown is beautiful. Tricia smiles and moves her hair around her ear. It is a beautiful dress. Ken's mind starts to wonder about the possibilities that could have been with this woman in front of him. His stare at her becomes so intense that he fills chills all over his body, so he shakes it off. Ken, are you okay?

Tricia notices his stare and begins to blush a little. Oh, yes I am. I am sure that the leading man in your life is lucky as well! Ken starts to laugh to play it off. Not at all as lucky as you; there is no leading man in my life only hopes to find one.

Hey Tricia this is the dress that I would like to get but I want to make sure of the size first is there any way that I can find out and then reach out to you; I do not want anyone else to help me but you. Sure Ken, I can give you my card and you can give me a call.

Thanks you are a delight Tricia. My pleasure Ken! No, the pleasure is all mine! Tricia starts blushing! Let me get out of this dress and get my information for you. Tricia turns around and heads back into the fitting room.

Still seated in the chair in front of the mirror he starts to go into his thoughts while staring at himself in the mirror. Man, what am I doing? I can't cheat on my wife this way but I am sure that she has cheated on me as she has in the past.

While staring into the mirror he notices a small crack starting to form out of nowhere.
Zig Zag lines slowly start to wind its way all over forming what seems to be a figure. Ken rubs his eyes because he cannot believe what he is seeing. Crack, Crack

the sound of glass splitting makes him sit up straight and look around to see if anyone else notices, but he is the only customer in the building, the two other ladies are further to the front of the store.

Red eyes start to glow from within the cracks, the shape of horns takes form and a growl comes from nowhere. Ken starts to become terrified but is stuck in his fixation. Curiosity makes him get up from the chair and walk over to this mirror slowly; he wants to make sure he is not seeing things.

Ken stretches out his hand to touch the mirror and all of a sudden a black mass darts out at him making him trip backwards in fear falling to the floor. Quickly he picks himself up and glances back toward the mirror while Tricia walks out of the dressing room with gown in hand. You okay Ken? Your mirror is cracked! Which one? The mirror over here to the right just cracked.

Tricia looks over to check it out and sees no trace of broken glass. I don't see anything Ken; it must have been a smudge you saw. Ken wipes the sweat off of his forehead and takes a deep breath. I hate to say a quick bye to you Tricia but I really need to be getting back. Okay Ken!

The two walk toward the front of the store and Tricia gives him her card. Ken reaches for the card and gives her a lingering touch on her hand before taking the card from her.

I will give you a call as soon as I get those measurements. Okay, you have a wonderful day! You too Tricia have a great day, ladies same to you as well. Ken nods his

head in their direction and walks
out the door.

Chapter 3
When Jealousy Goes Wrong

Ding, Dong! The doorbell rings and then is followed by a knock. I'll get it Ken; Key granddad is here to pick you up for the weekend! Sam makes her way down the flight of stairs through the dining room to the front door.

Hi Dad! Hey sunshine Sam! Come in dad Keyvon is almost ready, you know he has to pack his favorite toys for the stay. Francio or Frank for short is a handsome older man in his early sixties although nicely built for his age; he had knee surgery about 3 years ago, which has him walking with a cane.

Well, Well Sam, what are you so dolled up for? Sam closes the door behind her father and locks it. I have a meeting to go to this afternoon the Vice president of the company is coming in from Florida, kind of a meet and greet.

Ken walks through the threshold of the living room with Keyvon trailing behind him holding on to his spider man action figure; over hearing Sam telling her father about her meeting, as his face turns sour. I didn't know that you had a meeting today Sam, I thought we would go out and grab a bite to eat or something, you know make a day out of it.

Oh, sorry Ken I forgot to tell you about it, it was so abrupt we found out about it yesterday, it completely slipped my mind to tell you about it; it should only take about a couple of hours, we can go out when I get back. Sam manages to fold her lips into a half smile.

Hi dad, how have you been? Oh, I have been good this knee of mine has been giving me a hard time but other than that ken I am well. How is Mom doing? You know her, when I left she was up in the kitchen cooking Keyvon's favorite dish ravioli. Frank looks over at Keyvon and passes him a smile. What you got there Key?

My spider man Grandpa! Well you sure are holding spider man very tight, you sure he can breathe little man? He is protecting me Grandpa. Really, Key; who is he protecting you from? The dark mean stranger that sits in my room, that makes me scared. Frank's face turns into confusion as he listens to his grandson speak of the dark stranger.

Have you been watching scary movies little man. No Grandpa. Kenny kneels down to his son and places his hands on his shoulders. Key, we will not let anyone or anything hurt you okay, nothing is there son.

Kenny becomes a little unnerved listening to his son telling the story of the dark stranger because he knows that something is not right but he can't make out what is going on.

Sam raises her brow while listening and wants to speak on it but is afraid that no one will believe her as well besides, she doesn't want her son to be more afraid than he already is. Keyvon it is okay sweetie nothing is going to hurt you baby; now you grandpa and grandma are going to have so much fun this weekend; mommy and daddy are going to be so jealous but will miss you lots okay. Okay mommy. Key walks up to his mom and gives her a hug and a kiss. I love you!

Hey dad I will walk you and Key out to the car with his bag. Okay son thanks. Kenny puts his cell phone down on the dining room table grabs key's bag and then takes a hold of his hand. Sam watches as the three of them walk down the driveway to the car pausing for a minute due to their conversation.

Curiosity takes a hold over Sam as she glances over to the dining room table at Ken's phone, so she closes the door walks over to the table and picks it up. I know he is up to something; she can't help to think to herself.

Sam quickly starts to scroll through his call log to see if there are any new names or numbers she doesn't know about. Tricia! Who the hell is Tricia? Sam peeks around the door and through the window to see where they are standing and notice that they haven't even made it to the car yet; then quickly presses the number 1 button on the phone to see if she can get into his voice mail.

"Please enter your code". Sam thinks of the most common 4 numbers her husband uses. She tries the last of his social. "Please try again," the message says. Sam then uses her son's birth year. "You have two new messages, and one Saved message." The saved messages play first.

Hey Ken, this is Tricia I saw that you tried to call me sorry I missed you; I look forward to hearing from you, until then! "To save this message press 9!"

The message on the phone prompts in. Sam presses 9 to save the message, quickly hangs up and places the phone back on the table as she hears the door start to open.

Kenny walks into the dining room and sees Sam acting strange. You okay Sam? Oh, I am just fine. Ken reaches in to give her a kiss and she pulls away from him. Okay, I will be back soon I don't want to be late for this meeting. I should be back in a couple of hours ken. Well, I have some errands to run today anyway that will keep me busy until you get back.

Sam rolls her eyes at Ken. I'll bet you do! Hey what is that for Sam? I'll see you later Ken, I have to go. Ken's face begins to turn a light shade of red tightens his bottom jaw and clenches his teeth. Damn, she is really starting to get on my nerves.

The front door slams behind the clicking of Sam's heels on the stairs leading to the driveway, while ken watches his wife walk hastily to her car, he can't help to think to himself if this surprise that he has set up for her is really worth all of the trouble.

Ken turns to pick up his phone on the way to go upstairs to finish getting dressed for the day, when he notices his phone has a voicemail that he hadn't listened to; it was simply a bill collector. The phone then goes into saved messages.   Ken listens to the voicemail left by Tricia.

Ken's face turns up a smile listening to her voice; so kind, warm and inviting verses the nagging, condescending tone of his wife.

That's strange! It was under saved messages I haven't heard this message before and I didn't save any messages either. Kenny shrugs it off and resaves the message then decides that he needs to give her a call.

Click! Tic! Kenny turns quickly from hearing noise from his right side, so he looks in that direction. He sees nothing but notices on the red oak cabinet in the corner nestled by the closet door; sat a picture of him and Sam on their wedding day.

Ken walks closer to the picture in disbelief. How could? What in the world? Ken stops in front of the picture. The picture that was once sitting upright and on its kickstand is now standing upside down and at an angle leaning, with only a corner of wood from the cabinet supporting it.

Grrrr! Ken hears a low growl as if a dog where standing in front of him ready to attack him. Fear is struck into his heart like a spark igniting a wild fire in a desert terrain.

Ken decides to skip going upstairs because he knows for a

fact that they didn't own a dog and that he wasn't imagining the growl so he quickly grabs his keys on the wall hanging off the key holder and races towards the door.

Caught in the act

Sam parks her car and picks up her phone to make sure to let him know that she has made it to Carabas and that she would be in shortly. While flipping down the sun visor she reaches into her purse and pulls out her lip-gloss, which smells like, chocolate but shines like the morning dew kissed by sunlight.

Humph! Who the hell does he think he is messing with, obviously he doesn't know; I can show him better than I can tell him. All at once Sam jumps at the sight of a black Smokey mass passing across her mirror; so she turns around quickly to see what it was.

The time is near. A low like raspy whisper is what she hears, so Sam throws her lip-gloss into her purse rips the keys from the ignition and hurries out of her car. The sound of cars driving by as well as construction drowns out the sounds of birds sitting, in the neatly cut bushes lining the sidewalk.

Sam reaches the front door of the building but steps aside trying to let two customers who are exiting the building through the door first. The man lets his wife through the door and lingers to hold the door for Sam. Thank you. Sam smiles and walks in scanning the dining area looking for her friend.

Mmmm, there he is, she notices John sitting at the booth on the far right hand side of the bar with a window view. John was a handsome man but not as handsome as Ken by far; he was very clean cut, 5'8, and around 155 in weight. John is the CEO of Havana's Goods a distributor for various food products.

John knows that Sam is married but doesn't care because he is not looking for a commitment anyway, his lifestyle doesn't permit him to become too involved with anyone. Sam smiles in his direction while walking toward the table. The sound of silverware and plates clicking fill the air, while unclear chatter stirs in the room.

John rises from his seat to greet Sam. Hello Samantha, you look great. Thank you John so do you. Sam takes her seat on the other side of the table and John follows suite.

May I interest you guys in the house special today? The waiter smiles at the two sitting in the booth and introduces himself. My name is Trevor and I will be your waiter today. Hi Trevor! John looks up at the waiter and acknowledges him.

No thanks, I would like a corona and water for a drink; Sam do you know what you would like to drink? Sam raises her head from the menu and smiles. Yes, I would like a corona as well thank you. The waiter nods his head at the two of them and places the silverware on the table in front of them.

Would you like a minute to decide on your course? Yes, thank you. Okay I will be back to take care of you guys in a minute as well as to bring your drinks. Thank you Trevor!

So Sam, how have you been? I have been okay John, just working a lot trying to keep up with the new inventory that is coming in. How have you been John? Work is work you know! I just got back in town when you called. Really, what far off place were you dabbling in this time?

I had to go to Japan for about Three weeks to try and pull in some new clientele. Did everything go according to plan for you? Well you know Sam; I always get what I want. John looks up at Sam and throws her a wink. Sam, you really look good today! Well thank you John, I make it a point to stay on point. Yes you do Sam, you sure do.

The waiter walks up to the two in the middle of their laughter. Here are your drinks. You guys ready to place your orders, or do you need a little more time? I'll have Shrimp Weesie and a Caesar salad. Sam closes her menu and hands it to the waiter.

That sounds good; I will have that as well. John folds his menu closed and hands it off to the waiter as well.

I hate to ask but I must, how are you and the husband doing? Please don't ask me about him john, I can't even stand to think about him right now. I only ask because we are friends, although you can always drop him and get with a real man. John pokes his chest out a little more as if he is starting up a mating call.

Sam wants to laugh so bad because she knows in her heart of hearts he has nothing on her husband. The only reason she is even entertaining him is because she feels like her husband has lost his lust for life; she craves excitement and she just hasn't gotten it from her husband, so she goes on dates with other men.

Sam figures that she knows now that he does still have a lust for life, but that the lust is after someone else. Yeah she has been on dates but she has never slept with anyone of them.

Sam feels sick to her stomach just to think about another woman touching and loving her husband, she doesn't notice that she has a blank stare on her face.

Hey Sam you okay over there? John grabs a hold of her hand and caresses her fingertips. Oh, I am sorry John I don't know where my mind was, you were saying? I wasn't saying anything at all Samantha; I'm just trying to make a little conversation with you.

I'm sorry John I guess the stress is starting to weigh me down, any way tell me about your trip to Japan.

Sam knew that once she asked him about himself that he would talk what seems like forever. You know Sam you are a very special lady, you should let me show you just how special.

Meanwhile:

Kenny decides that he will instead of calling Tricia, he would just go up to the store to see her; he knows Sam's dress size from taking a peek in the closet; he also thought that it would be nice to just see her.

Ken's feelings for his wife are now sour after how she treated him this morning; he needed something to cheer him up. Damn, this traffic is rough today. There was construction going on everywhere it seems.

Ionia

The streets were being repair from all of the pot holes left behind from the harsh winter snow. Kenny decides that he would try and find a quicker route to get to the bridal store, because he knows with the heat that he is feeling from the sun and the frustration of people driving as if they can't drive would be a mixture for disaster.

Yeah, I can take a left on Fuller I can bypass most of this congestion if I turn left at the next light. Ken puts on his left blinker to try and butt his way in to the left lane. The sound of a horn billows in the air. Hey watch it you idiot! Ken looks up in his rear view mirror and notices the driver behind him giving him the finger. Thanks man! Ken smiles. Ken reaches over to turn the radio up after he comes to a halt at the light.

Melisha Ross

When he turns his head and sees what looks like Sam seated by a window at Carrabas. That can't be her. Ken squints his eyes a little to get a better view.

That is her; she was supposed to be at the office. Ken inches the car up just a little but not enough to hit the car in front of him so that he can get a better look. Who the Hell! Ken sees that his wife is not by herself but with another man. Ken has become heated and worst of all the light has now turned greens so he has to move.

Ken makes the left hand turn and then manages to make a U-turn to an adjacent parking lot so he can watch from a distance. The heat from the sun is in no comparison to the heat from the rage that he is feeling at this moment. He watches as the stranger sitting next to his wife grabs a hold of her hand and starts to caress her fingertips.

Ken has enough of watching his wife being touched by another man, so he puts his car in reverse and heads back to the house. The party is off, she is not deserving of anything.

The more insane part of his mind wants to go back and go into the restaurant and confront his wife; but he decides not to because his pride is too shattered and the strongest part of his manhood wants to break down and cry.

Ken starts to devise a plan in his head to catch his wife in her lies; he decides to carry on and take her to the movies and act if as nothing has happened at least for the time being. There is more than one way to skin a cat.

Sam breaks away from her stare and notices that John now has her hands caressing her and is leaning in for a kiss. Sam clears her throat and politely moves her hand back from his grasp. *Oh I'm sorry I don't know where my mind was what were you saying?*

After a couple of minutes of John going on and on about himself, the food has finally arrived. Here you are Sr. and Ma'am. The waiter places the food on the table and picks up the empty bottles of coronas. Is there anything else I can get for you guys?

John looks over at Sam, Sam shakes her head no. Not at this time Trevor we are okay, thank you! No problem Sr. So Sam we have known each other for about a couple of months now, when do I get to know you on a more personal level? Sam smiles with a slightly disgusted grin and shove some food in her mouth.

John smiles at her thinking that she is just being bashful. Lady you can run but you can't hide! John starts to laugh because in his mind he is *God's gift to any woman and no* woman would refuse him.

The two finishes up their meals and John picks up the check. Sam cannot wait to get away from him. When will I see you again Sam? Well, John I will call you when I am free. The two share a hug and part ways.

Mr. Murphy, are you sure about this? Yes Tonya I am sure, we've had a situation that has come up and we will not be having the party; please cancel the banquet hall and hotel room, maybe I can get the deposit back from them, oh! Don't worry I will still give you full payment for your time and efforts.

Mr. Murphy, I am truly sorry that things have taken a sudden and unexpected turnaround; I do hope that everything works out for you however. Thank you for your kindness Sharon.   No problem at all Mr. Murphy.

Ken hangs up the phone and takes a seat on the living room couch and breaths in deep. Thoughts of his wife sitting in the window are racing through his mind making him feel exhausted mentally.

With his eyes closed to relieve some of the pressure from the headache now forming starting at his temples; The front door starts to open followed by the sound of high heels clicking on the last cement step before entering the threshold, breaks his relaxed position so he opens his eyes.

How was the meeting at the office Sam? Well hello to you too Ken. Sam walks over to the dining room table slips her heels off and tosses the keys on the table. It was long Ken, a lot of my co-workers asked how you were and told me to tell you hello.

Ken sits in an upright position on the couch with his hands intertwined. Really, that's nice; were they impressed with the way everything is going at the office? Who? You, know Sam the VIP. Oh, yeah I am sorry, forgive me I am just a little tired Ken.

Yeah, I'll bet you are tired Sam I'll bet you are! Sam glances over to Ken with confusion leaking from her eyes. So did you get those errands done that you said you needed to do Ken? Yeah I did, was a lot of construction going on all over the place though.

Sam takes a seat on the love seat across from Ken leaning back making herself comfortable. Yeah Sam especially over there on Fuller, I was stuck at that left hand turn for a minute because of the traffic.

Interest is now rising in her so she sits up a little taking more of a notice on where he is headed with this piece of conversation. All she could think to herself is surely he hadn't seen her sitting there with John; it would be too much of a coincidence for him to had seen them. They have really done some remodeling to that Carraba's there on the corner, have you seen the changes to it yet Sam?

Sweat starts to trace the side of her face; with hesitation she shakes her head. No I haven't been on that side of town in a long time Ken. Oh, well then we should go there for something to eat Sam, are you hungry at all? Not at the moment Ken, the VIP bought us some food today at the office.

So what did you have to take care of on that side of town Ken? Oh, well I had heard there was a great party store off of Jefferson St. Party store Ken, what for? Remember we have to start planning for Keyvon's birthday.

Smash! The sound of glass hitting the floor startles the two in the middle of their conversation. What was that? I don't know Ken. You stay here Sam I will go check. No I am going with you Ken, you're not leaving me in here a lone; we go together.

The two of the stand up with Ken leading Sam following holding on to his arm as they make their way toward the kitchen.

I don't see anyone. While inching closer to the kitchen, the two stop when they hear the crunching sound of glass under their footsteps. What on God's green earth happened in here!

Sam did you leave a glass out on the kitchen counter? No, did you? No I didn't, it looks like it was thrown at the window; look there is glass over there on the table and the window is cracked. Okay Ken I am getting a little freaked out now, let's just clean up this mess and get out of here.

Chapter 4
We've Hit Rock Bottom

Saturday July 2nd 2011

Ken is stretched out on the bed with remote in his hand, flipping through the channel guide trying to find something to watch. Keyvon is with his grandparents for the weekend so that Ken and Sam can finish getting preparations for his birthday party set up; they thought it would be good for him to have his first surprise birthday party.

With all of the excitement that is going on in the house it is still been hard for Ken to concentrate because he still has an unhealed womb from seeing his wife with another man. Yeah, he has walked around as if nothing has happened but inside he feels as if his soul is dying.

Ken checks for the time and notices that it's 9 o'clock p.m. I just need to get this off of my chest; I am tired of her living a lie. Ken places the remote on the side of the bed beside him and adjusts the pillows that are place behind his head. The bedroom door swings open with Sam darting through in a high-pitched voice.

Did you remember to get the plates and the party hats Ken? Of course I remembered to get them Sam I am not an idiot you know? Humph! You sure could have fooled me Ken! Sam cuts him a look that even the most evil being would have been scared of.

You know Sam I am so sick of the constant attitude that you give out day in and day out! Excuse me Ken; I am giving you attitude; that is not all I wish I could give you right now! Sam slams the dresser door after she picks out her nightgown. What are you saying Sam, what else do you want to give me?

Whatever Ken I am so sick of the arguing with you! Yeah and it has been a patch of blooming flowers with you Sam. Drop it Ken! No I will not drop it Sam! Okay since you want to keep this fiasco going while you are at it; tell me who the Hell Tricia and Tonya is! Sam pauses in front of the bed after waiving her hands around and about with anger and stares directly at Ken.

Ken stares back at her holding his gaze with hers. Oh, you think that you have everything figured out in your mind don't you Sam; While we are asking questions here, Who in the hell were you eating lunch with at Carraba's and who were you with coming into this house at 3:00 am, when you were suppose to be out with your friends?

Shock comes over her face as she breaks her stare with him. I don't know what you are talking about Ken. Don't you dare lie to me Sam, I saw you sitting there and I watched as he held your hand and caressed your fingertips. Tell me Sam; are you back to your cheating ways?

Why are you dodging my question Ken, do you have something to hide? Ken sits up in the bed and begins to laugh because it is the only thing that is keeping him from blowing up from the rage that is tearing away at his heart. Answer my question Sam! His laugh suddenly stops and starts spilling into a more aggressive tone.

Sam's face turns sour with a look of hatred, she knows that

she has been caught but doesn't want to admit to it. Who are they Ken! Sam's calm tempered voice turns into a yell.

You really want to know Sam, huh; well I will tell you who they are. Sharon is an events coordinator, who was helping me plan an anniversary party for me, oh and Tonya was helping me with the formal gown I had chosen for you to wear.

All that was called off however Sam, when I saw you at Carraba's. Ken picks up the cell phone laying on the nightstand by the bed and tosses it to the end of the bed towards her. Don't believe me, since you are into going through phones, call them and ask.

Sam's eyes start to fill with tears as she listens to her husband explain who the two women are, feelings of guilt race through the very depths of her soul. Sam covers her face with the palms of her hands. I am so sorry Ken, I thought you were cheating on me; I went out on dates with two men that I know but I never slept with them I swear.

Why Sam, Why would you do this? I needed excitement, I felt like you no longer felt a rush for life with me; the war has changed you a lot, I feel like I lost the man I married.

No, Sam you changed me when you cheated on me I have been going through this marriage trying to forgive you, but I guess I never really did. Sam walks up to her husband and places her hands on his chest. I want only you Ken, please forgive me. Ken looks into the eyes of his wife for the first time in a long time.

He sees the sincerity in her eyes, which causes great passion stirring within his body. Sam realizes that her husband is becoming anxious to have her, but she doesn't believe that he will follow through with it; it had been a long time since he had touched her in that way.

Ken grabs his wife by the shoulder still looking into her eyes he pulls her close. You want lust; you want heat, well that is what I am going to give to you.

Ken kisses his wife passionately on her lips running his hands through her hair, taking her in as if she would be his last breath. Sam feeling the closeness and the intoxication from his kiss returns the emotions to her husband. The two make love all through the night feverishly as if it was their first time.

A birthday to remember

July 3rd 2011 12:30 pm

The house is finally decorated with balloons and banners; the table was set with spider man birthday plates, hats, cups and napkins. Ken and Sam start to greet their guests as they start filing in.

The table is set to seat 13 children; they have games planned as well as the spider man action hero dropping in for a visit. The couple figured that since all of his little friends where from his daycare they might as well invite them all.

The doorbell rings. On the other side of the door stands Mrs. Janice. Ken opens the door to let her in. Hello there Janice so glad you could make it! Ken reaches closer to her and gives her a hug. I wouldn't miss this for the world.

Sam comes to the front of the house to greet Mrs. Janice. How are you Sam? I am doing good Mrs. Janice, how have you been? You know me Sam just working and enjoying every day I am here. Come on in Janice. Ken closes the door behind her. Okay everyone, we don't want to scare Keyvon so no loud out bursts okay! All the children in unison agree.

Sam goes back in to get the candles from out of the kitchen cabinet and places then on the kitchen counter, when her cell phone rings. Hello, hi mom, okay everything is ready. Sam hangs up the call and announces to everyone that the birthday boy is almost here.

Yay! The children all have excitement in their eyes awaiting his arrival. Ken peeks out the bay style window in the front of the house and sees his in laws pulling up the driveway. They are here, places everyone.

All of the children take a seat at the dining room table while Sam places the 3 candles on his spider man cake and lights them. Ken reaches over to the lights and turns them down low.

Frank opens the door holding on to Key's hand and Francis his wife follows behind them. Where are mommy and daddy? Key looks around for his parents. Come in here son we are in the dining room.

Key walks towards the dining room area and all of a sudden everyone starts to sing to him *Happy birthday to you, happy birthday to you, happy birthday dear Keyvon, happy birthday to you!* Sam walks out of the kitchen with his cake and places it on the table.

Frank helps him into the chair seated at the head of the table and places his hat on his head. Make a wish and blow out the candle sweetie. Sam takes a picture with the camera while Key blows out the candle.

Everyone in the room cheers as all of the candles go out. Key's eyes are   gleaming with joy, as he sits amongst his friends and eats cake and ice cream. Thank you mommy and daddy, this is the best day ever.

Ken and Sam leave the dining room area to sit in the living room to talk to their parents. Francis smiles as the two enter and sit next to her. Well I am glad we pulled this off Ken and Sam, he has been asking questions all weekend. Fran as her family calls her lovingly is very kind woman she stands about 5'4 smooth caramel skin and short salt and pepper hair.

Fran was very graceful, everything that she did had certain flair about it, from the way she walked even how she talked had people mesmerized. Fran had been through hell and back; her mother and father were alcoholics, they were never really there for her, so she basically raised herself; she made a promise that she would never do any children that she had the way they did her.

We are too mom! Ken looks over to Sam and gives her a wink. Ahh, looks like you two are doing better. Ken and Sam start to smile with a little embarrassment. Yes we are mom; we are doing a lot better. Ken puts his arms around Sam and kisses her forehead after finishing his statement.

The day was going great they played pin the tail on the donkey, the kids enjoyed pictures with spider man and they watched movies. It felt like nothing could go wrong that this was going to be the chance to turn things around starting with today.

A gush of wind goes straight through the house. Man! Did you feel that breeze is the doors closed Sam? Yes mom, all of the windows and doors are closed. That was like the arctic snow. Francis folds her arms and starts to rub them to shake off the chill.

Okay everyone let's move this party outside okay!
Ken gets up from the couch and heads towards the kitchen grabs a bag of charcoal and lighter fluid so that he can start up the grill.

Sam goes into the dining room where the children are seated and looks over the kids while they are finishing their plates. Who's ready to go outside and play! All of the children cheer with agreement and in one accord. Did you guys and girls bring your swimsuits? Yes! Good! Sam turns to the parents that were there helping out and smiles. Okay parents; let's get the kids suited up.

One by one the kids get into their swim wear and head outside to the miniature swimming pool that is set up on the side of the house. Some of the children decide they are not ready to go in but want to play on the swing set nestled in the far right hand corner of the yard instead. Ken takes his place behind the grill placing hot dogs and hamburgers on the racks. The aroma of the food starts filling the air as the sun beats down on every one and every object not protected by shade.

The adults are the last to come out of the house because they stayed inside to clean up some of the mess left behind from the children. So to get a little rest they all take a seat on the lawn chairs placed neatly along the yard in various spots.

Children's laughter fill the air, the sound of water splashing in the make shift pool is over riding the sound of the food cooking on the grill but not drowning out the smell of the meal being prepared. Ken, standing over the food holding his spatula looks up to basks in the happiness that he sees on his son's face while playing with his friends.

Sam walks up to ken to hand him a plate to place some of the meat that was ready to be taken off the fire. This has been a wonderful day Ken. Yes it has Sam. The two share a quick kiss.

Look at me mommy and daddy! Keyvon calls for the attention of his parents as he goes to walk up the stairs on the slide to the swing set made of oak wood. Be careful Key! Key, reaches the top of the slide, stands up so that he could place his legs in front of him; when a sudden burst of wind opens up the back door to the house, goes through the smoke created by the grill, carrying a trail of smoke traveling toward the swing set at Key and knocks him off the slide sending him plummeting to the ground.

Keyvon! No! Ken, and Sam rush to the swing set to see their motionless child lying on the ground with eyes closed. Someone call the paramedics!

Everything with an instance stops. One of the parents hears the cry for help, grabs her phone and calls 911. Sam is now crying hysterically.

Ionia

Keyvon! Keyvon! Ken tries frantically to get his son to open his eyes but has no luck. Tears start to flow like a lake pouring out to the ocean as Sam's heart ache finds a voice of sorrow which billows out from the pain that has become to unbearable to keep in.

Ken grabs a hold of his son's hand and talks to him waiting the ambulances presents. Frank and Francis run to their sides and kneel down holding Sam and trying at all cost to comfort and assure her that he will be okay, holding in their own pain as best as they can.

Key cracks open his eyes slightly enough to look up at his parents and with a soft voice speaks to them. Mommy, daddy it hurts so bad. Tears start to fall down his cheek as he speaks to his parents. I'm sorry. Then he closes his eyes as if going to sleep.

The ambulance arrives to the scene after about 5 minutes. The sirens are blasting through the neighborhood and the red and white flashing lights are reflecting off of the sides of the adjacent houses. I need for everyone to move back and give us some room please.

Three paramedics exit the van one from the back and the other two from the front. With a hurried motion they grab the gurney and duffle bags and assess the situation. One man leans over and checks him for a pulse. We have a pulse. The Second man notices that something is not right with his body.

He has a break in his neck. The third man places a brace around his neck carefully and the other two assists him with placing his limber body gently on the gurney and straps him in. Two of the men rush him into the back of the van. The third man stays behind. Which one of you would like to ride in the back with him? Sam, you ride with him; mom, dad and I will meet you there.

Sam hurries and jumps into the back of the van and sits at Keyvon's side. The doors shut closed and the van pulls off. Ken watches the ambulance ride down the drive way as he hears the sirens blaring still down the street dissipating with each street it travels down until it is heard no more.

The parents start to assist with the children who once was filled with laughter are now crying at the sight of their friend being hurt. Frank and Fran are rushing around getting the last guest out of the house, turning lights off and turning the grill off.

Frank sees Ken standing in the driveway with his hands cradling his face weeping like a newborn baby. Ken, it will be okay son, we have to be strong now we need to pray. Frank places his hands on his shoulders to comfort him while holding back his own tears. Fran walks out of the house with purse in hand locking the door behind her.

Which hospital is he going to Ken? They're taking him to Bloggett mom. Well let's go then baby. The three of them jump into the car and head towards the hospital putting on the hazard lights to indicate that they are in an emergency situation.

The hardest thing to do

It's been three long agonizing weeks for the Murphy Family.

Sam and Ken have been taking personal shifts between the two of them so that someone is constantly up for Keyvon and to make sure that someone is always there.

They have had a couple of scares where he had flat lined and now he has gone into a comma, the doctors made a decision to put him on life support to help assist him with his breathing. The worst thing had been confirmed he had broken his neck and is suffering from a concussion and bleeding to the brain.

Balloons, flowers, cards, and teddy bears sent from well wishers lined the room in support of him getting better. The staff had made it as comfortable as possible for Ken and Sam but understood that it would never be like home for them especially under such dire circumstances.

It is hard for them to see their son laying in the hospital bed with tubes going through his little frail body, but they knew that it was necessary and for his well being.

Ken sits up in the chair that he had pulled away from the window and placed by his son's bedside. The hospital had given him his own room that had a white curtain in the middle; normally there would be another bed on the other side but they had decided due to the events that had taken place they would reserve the room for him and his family.

The floors were cold as ice, cabinets with different medical utensils where labeled in case of an emergency. Ken kept the television, which was posted in the corner of the wall on Disney channel in hopes that it would trigger something, familiar.

Time was running into itself as Ken glances at the two-hand clock on the wall closest to the bathroom door. Ken grabs his son's hand and starts to talk to him. It was nothing of significance just chatter in hopes that his son would hear his voice and wake up.

Ken follows the rhythm of his son's chest rising and falling, he knows that it is the machine and not truly Key that is causing this but wants with all his heart to believe differently. Come back to us son, please! Ken places a kiss on his forehead.

The door to the hospital room slowly opens up and a man wearing a white jacket, scrubs pants and shirt under it, walks in. Mr. Murphy, I need to speak with you and Mrs. Murphy for a moment. Okay sure thing, Dr. Nelson; Sam went to the cafeteria to grab herself something to eat; she'll be back in a minute. Okay Mr. Murphy I will be back in about 15 minutes.

The doctor's face looks a little grim which Ken notices so he can't help feeling torn because he knows that what he has to say is not going to be good, so he tries at all costs to pull himself together and brace himself.

The door swings behind him as Dr. Nelson walks back out of the room.

Fifteen minutes have passed by when Sam walks into the room with two coffee cups in her hands; she has been up all night watching over Key and her face is starting to show from the bags accumulating around her eyes.

Anything Ken? No Sam not yet. He has got to pull through this, he just has to. Sam hands a cup to Ken while pausing to look into Ken's eyes. Ken places a hand on his wife's hand. I know Sam, I know.

Thank you for the coffee baby. You are welcome. The two take a sip and place their cups on the table next to the bed. The doctor came in while you were out; he said that he needs to speak with us. Did he say why Ken? No not yet Sam.

Sam's heart has now jump into her throat, feeling as if she can't breathe so she walks over to the other side of the bed, takes a seat and grabs a hold to Key's other hand. My baby.

Knock, Knock! Come in! The door to the room creeps open slowly with Dr. Nelson and a nurse following behind him. The nurse passes by Dr. Nelson and goes straight over to the Iv bag that is feeding fluids to Key while the Dr. pulls up a chair next to Ken and Sam.

I regret to tell you Mr. and Mrs. Murphy that Key doesn't seem to be getting any better, the only thing that is keeping him with us is the life support that he is on. We need for you to make the decision as hard as it is to take him off.

Sam instantly starts to cry with this news. Ken looks at him with confusion and pain in his eyes. You mean there is no hope Dr. Nelson? A tear traces Ken's cheeks as he breaths in deep as if to catch his soul from dying.

I am truly sorry, he has no significant brain activity; Key is no longer there, even if some chance of a miracle he does start to breathe on his own he will be in a vegetable stage for the rest of his life.

Ken gets up out of his chair and walks over to Sam and embraces her as if to shield her from a bad dream, all the while knowing that he needed to be shielded from it as well. Ken pulls her slightly away so that he can look at her. Sam, we have to let him go. I don't want to let him go Ken, he is my baby!

I know I don't want to let him go as well but we cannot let him go through this either; he will always be with us.

Ken turns to the Doctor with as straight of a face he could muster even though he feels as if someone has punched him in his stomach repeatedly. Dr., can you give us time to notify the rest of the family.

That is perfectly fine Mr. Murphy; we will have to sign the paper work. Okay, I will be back Sam let me take care of this you stay here with Key.
Sam agrees though deep down in her heart she doesn't want to go through with this decision but she knows that it is for the best.

About 30 minutes pass by as Sam is sitting by her son, the door opens up and Ken walks in. Sam I have it set up to where we have another couple of days with him. Thank you Ken! She reaches over the side of the bed and pulls the covers up over her son to keep him warm.

Ken picks up the hospital phone and starts informing family and friends of the tragic news; the hardest call that he had to make was to his in laws. He knew that they would take it just as hard as they are.

Key is their only grandchild and has become the light of their life so he asks if they can come by so that they can spend a little time with him.

Without hesitation they agree to meet Sam and Ken at the hospital as soon as possible.

How do we say Good-bye?

Tuesday July 24th 2001 3:00 pm

It's been what seems like the shortest two days of the Murphy's life neither Ken, Sam, Frank or Fran has gotten any sleep, especially with their knowing what looms over their lives by this particular day.

Dr. Nelson arrives in the room with nurses in toe. Frank and Fran had asked for the pastor of their church to be present so that they could pray over him as he makes his transition.

It is time. The doctor looks at the family and wishes that they did not have to go through such pain. Sam grabs a hold of Ken's hand for support, as the two of them walk to one side of the bed; Frank and Fran walk to the other side.

The doctor reaches over to the life support system and pulls the switch. The suction from the tube starts to become slower and slower. Key's chest rises and falls slightly after the support and tubes have been taken away.

The family begins to think that there is hope but that hope fades as his chest no longer rises and he flat lines.
Sam holds on to her son's hand a little tighter not wanting to let go, the sound of sobbing consumed the room, it's as if the

world had come to a sudden stop for them.

Frank holding on close to Fran who had become too engulfed in sorrow couldn't bear to look so with tears falling profusely she buries her face in his chest.

The doctor allowed for the couple to sit with him for just a little while longer. They took their last chance to caress the hair on his head, his face and his fingertips. They knew that this is the last time that they will be able to touch him.

After about 30 minutes of time the doctor comes back in to let them know that they have to take him and get him ready. Dr. Nelson takes the sheet from the bed and covers the remainder of his body from head to toe.

Sam and Ken exit out of the room with the heaviest of hearts looking back as if this was all a mistake that he is just sleeping.

The seed has been planted:

It's been three weeks since Sam and Ken have had to lay their son Keyvon to rest. Ken mostly sits around the house staring into space and Sam has been so torn with grief she cannot at times even make herself get out of the bed.

Sam pulls the covers over her head and holds her pillow tight sobbing beyond control, when she starts to feel a little nauseous. Ken! Ken, come quick please. Ken hearing his wife call for him rushes upstairs to see what is going on.

Ken opens the door to hear his wife moaning in pain. Sam, what's wrong babe? I don't feel so well Ken. Do you need for me to get you something Sam? My stomach hurts so bad, I have to.

Sam before finishing her sentence jumps out of the bed, bolts into the bathroom and raises the toilet seat. Gauging is heard all through the room.

Ken races into the bathroom behind Sam after hearing the noise and grabs the ends of her hair and pulls it out of the way for her. Sam, you have been throwing up a lot lately, maybe we should see the doctor. It's probably just nerves Ken.

Sam I know that we have been through the worst thing in our lives but I haven't seen you this way before; the last time I have seen you in this state you were pregnant with Keyvon. No, I don't think so Ken it might be stress. I tell you what I will be back.

Where are you going Ken? I am going to the store. Without saying anything else, he races out the room and out the house.

About forty-five minutes later Ken comes back upstairs with a bag in hand. Sam, baby I know that you are not feeling well but take this test. Ken takes the clear blue easy box out of the bag.

Okay Ken, if this will ease your mind I will take the test. Ken walks over to the bed and helps his wife up. Sam grabs the box from his hands and walks into the bathroom and closes the door.

About 3 minutes later Ken starts to pace the floor. Sam, you okay in there? Silence is all that is heard.

Sam baby, are you okay? Ken walks to the door because his

nerves are now shot. Ken reaches for the knob on the door when the door opens.

Oh my God, I'm pregnant!

Chapter 5
A Child Is Born

It's been five years since the birth of their daughter and almost six years for the death of Keyvon. The years have been tough for the Murphy's, even though they have had the love and laughter revisit their home with their daughter; they still felt the absence of Keyvon.

Ionia is what they named their precious little girl. Ionia is a very out spoken little girl with remarkable resemblance to her brother Keyvon. Many who come into contact with her says that she is smart beyond her years and that she seems like an old soul.

Somehow the Murphy's felt that she seemed different; not different as in a slow learner or

too hyper, different as in talking to the air. They knew that most children had an imaginary friend at some point but this was different...
What is this?

Ionia wakes up with a smile on her face, she wants to be the first one up so that she can sneak into the kitchen and gets a hand full of cookies from the cookie jar.

As quite as possible she makes her way down the hallway one tiny little foot after the other, stepping on her tip toes. Ionia reaches the top of the stairs and grabs a hold of the railing so she can make sure that she doesn't slide down the stairs.

Feeling a little bit dizzy she stops before going down the stairs and closes her eyes slowly then reopens them. Ionia is confused by what she sees once she opens her eyes. It was as if she had stepped into a world within a world.

Laid right before her very eyes was what seemed like a sheer but intangible film, she was not afraid of this sight but rather curious?

Amazed by the beauty of this film she stretches her hands out to trying to capture it with her fingertips. The film was like a shimmering green emerald gems from the ceiling to the floor. Without hesitation in her mind she steps through it.

At first glance everything seemed as if she hadn't left the stairs but as she gets to the bottom of the stairs, she starts to notice a grey mist just above the floor. Ionia hearing voices in the dining room becomes a little disappointed because she wanted to be the first down stairs.

Meanwhile:

Ionia

Sam and Ken come out of their room after seeing Ionia trying to sneak out of her room, so the two decide to follow suite to see what she is doing. Kenny wait, what is she doing on the stairs? Is she sleepwalking?

Doesn't look that way Sam; looks like she might be stretching. The two decide not to say a word but just watch her.

Ionia notices however that it is more than two voices it sounds like her mom and dad has company over. Ionia reaches the last step on the stairs and stops at the threshold and peeks around the corner; instead of seeing her parents at the table she sees a group of 4 seated in the chairs playing a game of cards.

There were 2 woman and 2 men seated across from one another with drinks set aside and cigarette smoke lingering in the air.

My mommy and daddy are not going to like all this smoke in their house. Ionia steps through the threshold staring at every one of them.

The groups of people startled out of their wits sit as quite as a mouse in hopes that she doesn't see them.

They start to whisper trying to be careful barely moving their mouths. Ionia feels like this is the rudest behavior she had ever seen. Can she really see us? Well of course she cannot see us. Ionia stars deep into their eyes. Well of course I can see and hear you. Who are you?

It was an odd group of people indeed. She couldn't help but look at them with a strange grin on her face. With a kind voice, a lady seated closest to the window speaks to Ionia with a smile on her face. Hello little one my name is Geraldine; might I ask what is your name?

My name is Ionia. Oh, that is a pretty name Ionia. Geraldine is a beautiful woman; she has long jet-black hair, skin as chocolate as a river of fudge and light brown eyes.

The remaining 3 all spoke at once. Hi, Ionia! My name is Todd; a short man dressed in a blue uniform with name tag on the left side of his chest, looks as if he had just gotten off of work.

What kind of outfit is that Todd? Well, I work on a car that is I use to work on cars. Todd scratches his head with confusion and continues. I remember being at work and something hit my head and well I haven't worked

on cars since. That sounds sad
Mr. Todd.

Ionia turns to lady seated closest
to her by the stairs and the
strangest thing was that she was
in a long white gown with
something covering her face,
there is a man seated right beside
her who was wearing a black
tuxedo that had white strips up
and down the jacket.

You look so pretty in your
dress! Ionia smiles at the woman
and leans on the wall. Hello my
dear my name is Lisa and this
man sitting next to me is my
brother Jacob. Jacob tilts his hat
forward with his fingertips. How
do you do little one.

Thank you; you are a sweet
heart Ionia. Are you getting
ready to go to the princess ball?
I'm afraid not dear.

Ionia

I and my brother Jacob were on our way to the church so that I could marry the love on my life, I remember it was snowing outside and it was very slippery, we were almost to the church but then… Lisa starts to cry.

Jacob grabs his handkerchief from his jacket and hands it to his sister. Jacob turns to Ionia and finishes Lisa's sentence. But then we never got there. You never got there! That is so sad. I'm sorry you didn't make it to the church.

Geraldine turns and faces Ionia. I my dear sweet child was lying in bed on a wonderful summer day with my family and friends surrounding me. I was just so tired, I knew that it was my time to go so I said my good byes to my loved ones and advised of my last wishes and my physical body went to sleep for one last time.

We are no longer a part of the living world like you Ionia. We are all dead. It is not safe for you here child. We have tried to keep it at bay for you and your family the dark one is still around you must go. We shall keep watch for you.

Ionia goes to ask more questions but watches as they dissipate into thin air. Ionia frantically looks around but only sees 4 people at a distance as if they were watching the whole conversation unfold; they then slowly turn around to walk away. Hey come back! She starts to walk toward them.

Ken and Sam still watching:

Sam she is talking to the air, it's like she is holding a conversation with multiple people. That's silly Ken, there is no one in the kitchen. I know that! How can this be explained she has to be sleep walking, but she has never done this before? Shh, Shh! Hush Ken she is walking now, let's follow her.

What was her name?

Two of the 4 people a man and woman who were walking away disappear through an adjacent wall without a trace, a third person a male standing about 6'5 evaporated through a window but the forth person, a female with short hair was still walking but her steps began to hasten. Ionia follows behind her. Wait, Wait!

The woman goes through a door that opened up in mid air. Ionia now a little nervous because she knew that there wasn't a door like that in her living room but she still decides to walk through it.

Ionia is shocked beyond belief; there was a field of flowers, tall green grass, crystal blue skies and birds chirping in a distance with the sun beaming down. Peering over the mass of beauty over a slight hill she sees the woman who was walking away from her.

Ionia starts to run at a fast pace. Lady, why won't you stop! The lady hearing the frustration in Ionia's voice turns around with a smile and stops.   Hello Ionia. Ionia looks at the lady with confusion. How do you know my name?

A smile crosses the lady's face as she grabs a hold of Ionia's hands and holds them in hers. Ionia glances over her face, she can't help but feel a since of sincerity mixed with sadness and joy within her eyes.

Ionia

Tall in stature the lady knows that she must seem like a giant to her so she lowers her body down to where she is slightly kneeling; giving Ionia a better view of her face.

Ionia notices the lady wearing glasses that are now sitting on the tip of her nose, her d bronze skin looks like a field of ready to harvest wheat. Why do you wear glasses? Well Ionia, I appear to you as I was in the physical world.

Ionia smiles at her with a hint of confusion. Who are you? Well my dear, I was with you the first time you were born. Now you're just being funny Mrs. Lady. No my dear you will understand soon what I mean; I was a very good friend of your mother when we were in school all the way up until. Well, I passed away.

How did you pass away? My heart stopped when I went to sleep and didn't wake up; but its okay dear, I am just fine. You on the other hand have a special gift but it is not safe for you to be here. But why is it not safe for me; it is so beautiful here.

Suddenly a cloud rolls over the well-lit sun creating an unfamiliar shadow. Ionia becomes a little uneasy as she watches a dark mist rolling over the flowers in a distance killing all in its path.

Ionia you must go my sweet heart; I will always be around, I am simply a thought away. Mrs. You never told me your name. So the lady bends Toward Ionia's ear and whispers her name. Shock comes over Ionia's face as she is told her name. She closes her eyes and wakes up in the bathroom of her house with her parents standing in front of her in disbelief.

Ionia you okay? Sam grabs a small face towel and dampens it with a bit of water from the sink and applies it to Ionia's forehead. Mom, dad! You will never believe what just happened to me it was so great!

Ken reaches out to his daughter and moves a strand of her long wavy dark hair from over her eyes. Tell us what happened. Ionia starts speaking of excitement over the events that just took place; she gets half way through her story when her father stops her.

Okay baby; Let's just get you over to the couch for a minute. Sam grabs a hold of her hand and the three walk out of the bathroom, back down the hallway and into the living room.

Ken places a pillow on the arm of the couch and places his daughter gently down so she can rest. Are you hungry? Yes daddy I am hungry. Good I will go and make us some breakfast.

I will stay with her here for a minute Ken and then I will come in and help you. Ken kisses his wife and daughter on the forehead then exists the room. Sam reaches over to the pillow behind her daughter's head. Its okay sweetheart you were just sleepwalking.

No mom I wasn't, I really wasn't. Oh by the way mom, she says hi. Who says hi Ionia? You know, the lady that you knew when you were in school, she said you were very best friends but then she passed away; she was so young. Sam's eyes start to fill with tears but she tries to hold them back.

It was weird though mom she said that she was with me the first time; the lady even knew my name.   I'm not sure what the first time means baby girl.

Don't cry mom she says that she is always with us we are just a thought away. Sam turns around quickly and calls out to her husband loud enough to send him running back into the room.

What's wrong Sam? Omg Ken! Sam gets up from her side and whispers to Ken. This can't be she wasn't even born then, I was in school when she and I met how could she know about her? Ken looks at his wife with concern. She can't be talking about.

Sam turns to her daughter mustering every bit of strength she can. Ionia sweetie it's okay baby, can you do mommy and daddy a favor; tell us what her

Name was? That's a crazy question, you gave me her name; well my middle name is after her. Her name is Angie.

Ken and Sam's jaws drop to the floor and immediately Sam turns to Ken crying and he in turn holds her.
Why so sad guys? Ken speaks softly to Ionia. That is your mom's best friend who died before we were even married.

Chapter 6
I Will Be Your Guide

It's been about 3 weeks since the incident that the Murphy family had. Ken and Sam have tried to rationalize in every direction on how it is that their daughter could possibly know about someone so long ago.

Even with much deliberation the two decided to keep it to themselves. Ken, we cannot tell anyone of what happened. I agree Sam, we don't want people to look her in a strange way, and it would hurt our little girl.

It's quiet in here what is she doing? Oh, she said that she was tired and wanted to take a nap, I will check on her shortly. A nap sounds real good about now doesn't it Sam?

Sam slightly laughs at her husband and then begins to take out a couple of pots from the cabinets.

Suit yourself my love, but a woman's work is never done. Well I'm going to go upstairs to lay down Sam, wake me in about an hour. Will do babe!

In Ionia's Room:

A gush of wind flows through Ionia's room, passing across her face forcing her to open her eyes. Ionia grabs a hold of her covers to tighten it against her body to shield her from the chill, when she realizes that the window to her room was not open.

The room was dark because of the shades drawn and lights were turned off to help her sleep better. Ionia cannot get past the feeling as if someone is staring at her, so she inches out of her covers slowly to where she is sitting up against the headboard of her bed.

Ionia gives her eyes a second to adjust to the light and then starts to scan the room. There is nothing on the left hand side of her bed so she continues over to her closet door and again she sees nothing there, the doors are even closed shut.

While scanning the room her eyes close in on an object seated in her princess cushion couch right beside her dresser drawer.

Are you comfortable over there? My mom and dad are always telling me that it's rude to stare at someone. I didn't think that you could see me yet, I do apologize. Out of nowhere an illuminating light starts to shine from head to toe of this object. The apparition slowly gets up and starts towards Ionia's direction.

Don't be afraid my dear I am not here to harm you. Ionia takes a closer look at the person; she notices that it is a man dressed in a white cloth, which flowed down to the floor. The man looked very young; he had dark brown eyes no hair and a beautiful radiant smile.

So I'm guessing that you are not an angel right? What makes you say that Ionia? Angels have wings, everyone knows that! Well you are correct in your observation little Ms.

My name is Troy! Troy why are you in my room? I'm always here and where ever you are. Did you pass away too Troy? Why yes I did Ionia. May I ask how you passed away? I passed by my own means; I just did not want to be in the physical life anymore.

When my soul left my physical body I had time to reflect on my life as I rested, to look at the many decisions that I had made, some of the decisions where good others were bad. He to come back, not as an angel however but something else gave me the opportunity.

We are all put here for a reason, not one person's reasons are alike. Many people fall off of their course of learning as well as faith. Our greatest quest that everyone has to face is our ability to love beyond all faults; all forms of ignorance or self love and last but never least the love of our creator. When we allow ourselves to forget about that love, it creates a threshold for negative energy. You see little one, there are souls around us that feed upon that negative energy and it makes them that much stronger.

Those souls don't want to love learn and grow spiritually, so they seek the opportunity to comeback by any means necessary. Troy takes a seat in mid air beside Ionia's bed, while Ionia leans in as if she is being told a secret.

Meanwhile Ken on the way for his nap hears Ionia whispering and stops in the hallway just before her door:

Have I met you before Mr. Troy? Yes you have Ionia, but it may have seemed like a dream. Everyone has a guide, someone who assists in Watching over us; when we pass away we get to meet those guides. In your case and like selected few you are able to see me now.

Mr. Troy If I tell anyone they are going to think that I am strange. Ionia people are always afraid of something they don't understand, you will in time decide to share your gift; no matter when I will always be there.

Ken clears his throat and taps on the door to alert Ionia that he is standing there. Hey princess can I come in. Sure daddy! Troy lifts a finger to his mouth letting her know not to say a word about him sitting there.

Is everything okay in here sweetie? Yes daddy, why do you ask? Oh, I thought I heard you talking to someone. Don't be silly daddy there is no one in here.

I'm still a bit-tired daddy. Ionia gives off a fake yawn for her father and looks in Troy's direction and sees him laughing, so she quickly lies down; to prevent from laughing herself.

Sure princess I will come back to get you in an hour. Ken shrugs off the conversation that he thought he heard and goes into his room to take a nap.

Troy's laughter comes to a halt as seriousness crosses his face. I need for you to be careful when you step into the land of the spirits okay. Okay I will troy. Remember the dark energy is always around waiting, just say my name. Okay Troy I will. Troy disappears in mid air.

Ionia beginning to feel a bit tired shuffles her body in-between the comfortable sheets of her bed and buries the right side of her cheek into the soft satin pillowcase.

Maybe I will take just a short nap. Her eyes become much heavier than they were a minute ago so she closes her eyes and falls fast asleep.

Chapter 7
A Dream To Remember

Ionia dreaming:

Where am I? Ionia stops to take a look at her surroundings, for some reason everyone seems to be moving in slower than usual motion. Ionia knows that she is standing outside on a sidewalk with the sun beaming down on her face but she is unsure about where exactly she is.

A man walking on the same path that she is standing on wearing a business suite walks straight through her without saying a word. Well excuse me Sir! The man doesn't flinch at all it's as if she isn't even standing there.

This is very different for her; she must not be in the spirit world because the spirits at least can see her. Ionia notices that she has stepped into some shade so she looks up to see what was causing it.

Humph, it's some sort of cement over pass. Ionia turns around to see where it is coming from, she notices at the beginning of the over pass stands multiple glass windows and sliding doors with people coming in and out of it.

A sign to left hand side of the door reads: *Blodgett Hospital.* It had many arrows on it with one arrow in particular pointing straight ahead reading emergency room.

Ionia does not understand why she feels like something is pushing her in that direction so instead of fighting it she begins to walk towards and crosses over the threshold to the building, as the doors swing open.

Ionia

This was all new to her she'd
known that at one point in her
life she had been to the doctor's
office but she had never been in
an emergency room before.
Ionia's head turns quickly from
hearing the sounds of sirens
blaring in the air.

Ionia steps aside leaning on the
front desk where the receptionist
is seated typing away, with an
elderly woman barely standing in
front of her being seated in a
wheel chair because she has run
out of breath.

Ionia glances over to her with
concern on her face as the lady
takes I a deep breath looks into
Ionia's eyes, smiles and then
winks at her.

Ionia is puzzled at this point
because she didn't think anyone
could see or hear her. The double
doors slide open with two
paramedics and a gurney

carrying someone that she can't quite see, she could only see that it's a little boy with something around his neck.

While trying to take a glance at this little boy she hears a woman's cry following suit behind the paramedics. Ionia could only get a glimpse of the back of the ladies head that had long flowing wavy black hair.

After seeing the hurried scene that unfolded right before her eyes, Ionia turns to the lady seated beside her once more with a sad look in her eyes. That is very sad to see Mrs. Yes it is little one, there is something you must see go to level 3 room 303. We will see each other again.

Before Ionia could question the elderly lady a woman wearing a blue uniform she could still hear the lady coughing and gasping for air wheeled her off to an elevator.

Her heart sank in her chest for the lady, she hoped that she would be okay but felt like she would not be. Even still her heart was heavy because whatever the lady told her that she needed to see could not be good.

With hesitation in her steps she makes her way to a side hallway where a sign says *elevators*. The elevator doors open up and she is faced with an image of herself in the likeness of the funny mirrors like the ones at the local circus her parents had taken her to last year.

Reluctantly she steps through the door turns around and presses for level 3. It's not that Ionia is by any means cluster phobic but she can't help but feel as if she is being watched.

Ding! The elevator comes to a halt and she takes a step through. Up until now she hasn't noticed that she is not wearing any shoes until her toe touch the ice-cold white marvel floor.

The atmosphere was different here; there was fog lingering along the walls and all over the floors; white curtains were dangling and swaying as if they were on a clothesline outside in the wind.

The sound of screeching wheels from hospital beds being pushed back and forth through the halls all but in gulf the air, while faint beeping noises where heard in a far distance, which seemed to have a pulsating rhythm. Ionia wasn't quite sure of what the noise was for so she shrugs it off and continues walking towards the room number she was told to go to.

Ionia

Ionia passes by door 300 and stops to take a peek because it is left wide open, a deep sigh comes out as she notices the elderly lady that she had just seen in the lobby is lying in bed with tubes coming out of every which way of her body and her family and friends surrounding her.

The pace of her footsteps quicken from the sound of crying coming from about 3 doors down. Ionia reaches the door and pushes it open.
The image that she sees is very gloomy the atmosphere reeks of sadness and pain.

In her mind she cannot believe what she sees next because it is beyond anything that she has experienced until now. Mommy! Mommy! Ionia sees her mother with her hands over her eyes sobbing beyond control.

Ionia moves closely because she feels as if she may just be speaking too softly and she wants to console her mother. Thrown back from what seems like a gush of air she stands aside and notices that her dad and grandparents rushing in to be at her moms side.

Tears start to trace Ionia's cheeks as she watches her parents sit at the bedside of this little child. Time seems as if it slips inward and outward as she watches doctors and nurses come and go. The nametag reads Dr. Nelson. Ionia thinks to herself that he must be the main doctor because he comes in more frequently than the others.

Ionia hears:

I regret to tell you Mr. and Mrs. Murphy that Key doesn't seem to be getting any better, the only thing that is keeping him with us is the life support that he is on. We need for you to make the decision as hard as it is to take him off.

Ionia instantly starts to cry as she hears the conversation unfold. Many thoughts begin to run through her head questions like: could this be the death of her big brother that she was told about? Is this just a dreamt up vision of what she thinks happened with him?

Ionia never really understood the reason why she hasn't run across her big brother, she does talk to those that have passed on; so why not him? With every stroke of her parent's fingertips over the little boy's skin she felt and it was beginning to scare her; she hears every whisper they tell him.

The oddest thing happens to her next, she watches as her dad holds her mom and her grandfather holds her grandmother while the doctor flips a switch on the side of the bed.

A loud, long and continuous beep is heard in the air. Instantly Ionia is pushed towards the bed and into the little boy's body and Ionia opens her

Eyes to see her parents looking down on her, but they don't see that it's her and they cannot hear her. Ionia has an urge to close her eyes and fall to sleep so with a deep breath she closes her eyes.

Like a feather being lifted by the wind she feels fingertips reaching under her and lifting her up carrying her; she opens her eyes to see that it was Troy holding her in his arms.

Where are we going Troy? I am taking you away from this moment of time it is not safe here. Ionia turns her head to look back at her parents and see a dark entity standing over the little boy's body ready to jump in but is interrupted by an angel with beautiful wings with love and light spreading all around it.

The angel fends off the snarling dark force, which looks like a cross between dog and dragon with red eyes and long claws with the ability to stand on its hind legs. This dark force had wings that looked as if they had been burned and dipped in blood.

It was a fight indeed but she watched as the angel shielded him off. Troy looks down at Ionia and sees the terror in her eyes. Ionia do not watch what is going on; that is the darkness I am protecting you from, you must awaken and get out of here.

Troy puts Ionia down slowly on her feet and tells her to go back the same way that she came and to do it quickly. Ionia agrees to do as she is told and starts back down the hallway that she came, when she is stopped at door number 300 once again.

Beep... That long beeping noise she had just heard is now coming out of the room with the elderly lady. Ionia takes a pause and peeks into the room. Everyone in the room is now crying and gazing over the elderly lady.

Ionia watches as the soul of the elderly woman lifts from her body her hands being held by a man guiding her out. She could tell that it was someone that the lady was familiar with by the smile and gleam in her eyes.

Elderly woman:

Ionia

*I've waited for you all these years, it
is so good to see you; I've missed you
my dear.*
*Man: I told you I would wait for
eternity; come with me my dear*
*Elderly woman: I would follow you
from here, to the moon and back and
all eternity*

Ionia listens to the couple and
before the couple goes away, the
elderly lady turns to Ionia smiles
and winks. I told you that I
would see you again my little
one. We'll be watching over you.

The couple disappears into thin
are as Ionia wakes to the sound
of her dad calling her name to
wake her up from her hour nap.

Ionia, Ionia! Wake up princess,
look at you, you are sweating
beyond belief; are you Okay?
Ionia slowly opens and adjusts
her eyes before saying a word.
Daddy I had the craziest dream,
but it seemed so real!

Oh yeah, do you feel like talking about it princess? Yes daddy it was about my brother. Ken tilts his head with confusion. Your brother, ... what do you mean? Ionia starts to explain the dream to her father but is interrupted by him shouting out Sam's name. Sam! Sam! Come upstairs please!

The sound of hurried footsteps stomping on the carpet floor becomes louder and louder as Sam reaches the bedroom door. What is it Ken? You have to listen to this Sam. Ken turns to his daughter as Sam takes a seat next to him on Ionia's bed.

I need for you to start from the beginning please Ionia. Sure Daddy. Ionia starts from the beginning of the dream and explains in great detail all that she saw, the faces on her parents went from a look of concern to having multiple question, sadness and fear with each word that forms out of her mouth.

Ionia reaches the end of her recount of the dream and is met with silence lingering in the air. Pop! All three jump up from their position as the light bulb on the ceiling crumbles to the floor.

A shadow creeps over head in the still dark room as Ionia looks up and sees a dark mass her face starts to tremble. A bolt of light comes through the door of her room as she notices that it is Troy, he grabs the dark mass and disappears into the closet.

Sam and Ken watches their daughters' head move about from the door to the ceiling and in the direction of the closet in fear. What is it Ionia? Ionia notices her parents watching her so she pulls herself together. They wouldn't believe her anyway is what she is now thinking.

Nothing I'm okay. Ken looks up at where the bulb was. It must have swelled and exploded from being too hot. Sam chooses to agree with him for the sake of trying not to scare their daughter even though they are scared out of their wits.

You don't believe me do you mommy? Sam clears her throat and thinks of what to say to her before answering. That indeed was a very detailed dream princess very life like as well; oh I forgot princess grandma and grandpa are going to be here in about an hour.

Really where are we going mom? Remember they are taking you to the John Ball zoo today. Excitement lights up Ionia's face instead of the tension that at once had a hold over the atmosphere.

Am I staying over their house tonight? Yes princess you will be there until Sunday night.

Come on sweetie let's get your bag packed so you can be ready when they get here.   Okay daddy. Sam runs into the linen closet at the top of the stair, grabs the broom, dust pan, returns to the room and sweeps up the glass pieces.   Ken uncovers his daughter and helps her into her little pink princess slippers.

Honk! Honk! 30 minutes a horn sounds in the air and less than 2 minutes a knock is heard throughout the house followed by the doorbell. Sam hearing the doorbell, places the glass of water she had just fixed on the kitchen counter and heads toward the front of the house.   I'll be right there.

Sam reaches the front door and opens it to a pair of smiling faces.

Hi mom, Hi dad. Come in. Francis gives Sam a hug and kiss before stepping completely in the door. Hi Sam! Hi dad. So is our little princess ready to go? Yeah she is ready to go.

Thump, thump, thump. Everyone turns their attention towards the back of the house because they know that it's Ionia racing down the stairs to see her grandparents. Sam can't help but to feel overjoyed because during the loss of Keyvon they had become the glue that held her and her husband together from having a nervous breakdown.

In fact there were times when everyone thought she was going to miscarry Ionia; due to the stress that she was under the doctor had placed her on bed rest. Ionia is definitely a miracle baby. Grandma, Grandpa! Ionia's eyes are gleaming with excitement because she knows that every time she is with her grandparents   they are sure to have fun that follows.

Hello Ionia my sweet. Frank opens his arms wide so that he can receive her with a hug; he can't help but remember how Keyvon use to greet him in the same manor. Have you been a good girl for your mom and dad? Of course I have grandpa. Ionia grins and plants a kiss on his cheek.

How's grandma's little princess today? Francis grabs a hold of Ionia's face and stars deep into her eyes with a smile beaming on her face. I'm okay grandma. Francis kisses her on the forehead and releases her hands from her face.

Frank looks over to Sam and Kenny and leans on the wall just inside of the front door, crosses his arms and observes them before speaking another word to them. You guys okay? With a confused look on both of their faces they look at each other and shrug their shoulders.

We're okay dad every day is progress. Okay son, just making sure. Frank glances over to Francis and gives a slight smile because he knows that they are still having a hard time dealing with the loss of Keyvon. Frank knew that it had to be still the same fresh pain as the day he died especially, when looking at Ionia. Ionia is the spitting image of him it was just so uncanny, it had to be hard for them.

Okay Ionia let's hurry we have a movie to catch! Francis picks up Ionia's princess backpack filled with clothes and toys for her weekend stay. Ionia turns looking past her parents and notices Troy standing behind them. You take care of them for me while I'm gone okay. Troy flashes a simple wink. I will little one.

Everyone immediately stands still and looks in the direction Ionia is talking to but sees nothing. Frank looks over to Sam baffled because it was the strangest thing he had ever seen in his life. Well okay, someone has an imaginary friend I see. Troy is not imaginary grandpa that would be silly, he is my guide.

Francis decides that she should break up the awkward situation so she takes a hold of Ionia's hand. Let's go my dear, plenty of fun to be had. Yay! Let's go! Frank, Francis, and Ionia walks out of the house and toward the car, while Ken and Sam watches and smiles.

What could it have been?

The next night Sam and Ken had just returned home from taking in the sights and dining out at a nearby Blues Club on Market Street. Sam had done her fair share of drinking so Ken had to be the designated driver. Sam is finding it hard to walk in a straight line let alone up the stairs to the bedroom so Ken picks up his wife in his arms and carries her up the stairs.

Oh Kenny darling you don't have to carry me all the way up the stairs. Kenny starts to chuckle under his breath because her words are slurred, she's sounding like a schoolgirl, and for that matter she is singing the words as well. Hey honey I heard ya laughing at me Mr., what's so funny? Nothing Sam, nothing at all is funny.

The two reach the room and Ken sits Sam on the bed and

begins taking her red open toe
stilettos off. Oh I can take my
own shoes off Ken, I'm not a
baby you know. I know you are
not a baby Sam but. Sam reaches
over and moves his hands out of
the way, reaches down to take
her shoes off and almost falls off
the bed. Ken catches his wife
before she falls and places her
back up right.

See Sam, just let me help you.
Sam's face turns sour letting the
liquor poor negative thoughts in,
destroying the good times and
memories. You couldn't help
with Keyvon could you? Sam
puts her head down as tears fall.

That's not fair of you Sam where
you were? Ken knows that most
of what she is saying is from the
liquor but he also knows that it
makes people tell what they truly
feel. The last piece of clothing is
off of Sam so he lays her in
between the sheets, kisses her on

the forehead and proceeds to undress himself and lay next to her.

Meanwhile:

Frank had just finished reading Ionia chapters in her favorite book "The Never-ending Story", as he looks over and sees her fast asleep. Quietly he closes the book cuts off the light and walks out of the room trying not to wake her.

Sam is now sleeping though is having what seems to be a nightmare because she's tossing, turning and bumping into Ken waking him up every so often. The clock on the nightstand reaches 3 o' clock. Sam feels herself awaken but can't move, it is like something is weighing her down so she starts to panic.

Freighted she tries to scream but can't, she can't even at this point open her mouth to talk and she is unable to open her eyes to see, it's as if someone is holding her down to the bed.

Ken feels a vibration in the bed so he opens his eyes to see what is going on; glancing over to look at Sam he notices her body jerking stiffly and her hands clinched, so he rises out of the bed and turns on the lights.

With a frightened look on his face he tries to wake his wife but he can't though he hears her mumbling; At this point he thinks that she is having a seizure. God help me! Ken screams to the top of his voice. In an instance he sees his wife's body relaxes and her eyes slowly open while he is reaching for the phone.

Sam sits up as quickly as she can with quickened breath and her heart beating what seems like out of her chest. I couldn't get up Ken, I mean I was awake and could hear you but I couldn't talk, move, or open my eyes. What could that have been? I don't know Sam but it sure scared the hell out of me. Do you want me to get you some water? Yes please. Ken gets up gets some water for her.

Ionia's Dream

Mean while:
Ionia fast asleep dreaming of being in a castle having a tea party with her friends is interrupted when Troy walks in out of knows where. Ionia I know that you are having a tea party with your friends but your mother is in danger, you need to come quick! What do you mean Troy? My mommy is with my daddy. I know dear but the darkness is around her.

What can I do I am just a little girl and I'm scared. No need to be scared I will be with you, just use the love you have for her and I will be there every step of the way come on we must hurry.

Take me to her Troy, please! Troy grabs her little hand and the two journeys through what seems like a portal and she finds that she has ended up in her parent's house. It was dark throughout the house and a thin mist filled the air and covered the floor as the two of them make their way to the bedroom, they hear what sounds like growls from a dog. They pass through the hallway as Ionia notices the grandfather clock is chiming 3 o'clock. Ionia sees people going in and out of rooms and through walls but she is not frightened by them she is more afraid about what she hears upstairs.

They reach the hallway at the top of the stairs as she pauses and holds on tighter to Troy's hand. Its okay Ionia be brave, all it takes is a muster seed of courage. Okay Troy. Ionia breathes in deeply, as she begins to walk once more; until she reaches the door of her parent's room.

A look of terror crosses over her face as she sees a black mass with red eyes and horns from its dog like face hovering over her mother from the ceiling. The mass descends from the ceiling and places it's self over her mother as if it was trying to take over her soul.

Ionia watches as her mother is trying to move but can't, she is hoping that her father wakes up to help her.

Ionia sees her father awaken and she thinks that all is safe when she notices that he can't wake her either. Tears start to fall from Ionia's eyes because she doesn't know at this point what to do. So she lets go of Troy's hand and steps forwards and shouts at the dark entity. Leave my mommy alone!

The dark entity turns it's head in anger from being interrupted and roars loudly growling and snarling. Ionia's fear becomes anger because doesn't want this evil being hurting her mother so she closes her eyes while thinking of all the love she has for her parents and at the same time her and her dad speak the words. God help us!

Just like when a storm finishes, the rain stops, the sun shines a light comes out of nowhere crippling the demon just enough for Troy to step in and grab the entity pulling it away as the two of them disappears. Ionia stands there long enough to make sure her mother is okay then she wakes up in her grandparent's house.

Ionia awakes to see her grandparents standing over her with concern. You okay baby? We saw you struggling in your sleep then you said God help us? She must have had a bad nightmare Frank. I'm okay I just saved mommy. Okay, we are glad you did shrugging it off. You close your eyes and try to get some sleep it's still really early in the morning the sun hasn't even risen.

Frank and Francis turn the light out, after laying Ionia back to sleep and walks out of the room in disbelief. Ionia pretends to close her eyes but doesn't fall back to sleep because she notices Troy standing by her window seal. When she sees her grandparents are gone she reopens her eyes.

Are you okay Troy? Yes little one, he is getting stronger though, you my dear did a good job. You must be extra careful now because he is angry with you. I will always do my best to protect you okay. Okay Troy

I will, thank you for helping me. Your welcome Ionia now you get some rest I'll be here.

Chapter 8
A Much Needed Message

Sam and Ken haven't had much conversation about the event that happened recently. Though it was still bothering them they had seemed to let it go so Ken had thought. Sam was always on the computer or at the library looking things up but what it was Ken did not know, he had figured she was doing some kind of project for her job so he never bothered her.

It was Memorial Day weekend so Ken decided to take Ionia down to a local cemetery to place some flags on the graves of some fallen soldiers. Sam would you like to go with Ionia and me to the cemetery? Sam peers from around the computer and politely turns the idea down. You guys go I have some things to take care of here.

Okay we will be back soon then. Okay Ken. Ken grabs the small flags he had purchased from Wal-Mart a couple of days prior and he and Ionia head down to the cemetery on Kalamazoo and Alger Street.

He had picked this particular one because he had found out that it had a large amount of veterans there and he wanted to honor them for their service and he wanted his family to be a part of it.

Ionia helps her father gather the flags from the trunk of the car and the two head for the first site. The two read the names and dates on the tombstones as they place the flags on the side.

Ionia is becoming a little annoyed because everywhere she

looks there are people standing around asking her for help, these are not living people but people who have passed on.

She doesn't want to be insensitive to what they need but she just wants to spend time with her dad and they don't seem to get that she is ignoring them on purpose. Little girl tell my daughter I love her! Ionia looks at the lady standing in a conservative purple dress with purls around her neck but keeps walking.

Tell my best friend it wasn't his fault. Ionia smiles and the young man dressed in a grey suite with white stripes. A voice from behind a tree not too far from where she and her father are standing calls out to her. Ionia, granddaughters come here!

Believing it to be Frank and Francis she looks up and sees a man and a woman standing by the tree with warm smiles on their face. It's okay dear come here. Ionia turns to her daddy and asks him to look by the tree. Do you see them over there?

Who Ionia? There is no one here but us two right now.
Ionia realizes that the man and the woman are spirits and not of the living so she walks toward the tree. Ionia do not go where I can't see you! Okay daddy I will not, I am just going over here to that tree.

Who are you guys? We are your grandparent's dear. Really? Yes sweetheart, we have been gone a long time now from the physical world but it seems like yesterday.

We went on a vacation for the summer in Colorado, your daddy didn't want to go he wanted to go to a summer camp with his friends so we let him go there instead; well why we were there the stove caught on fire from some electrical issues, we didn't realize we left it on and then the place caught on fire.

We just wanted you to know that we have been watching over you.
Please tell your father that we are so proud of the man he has become. He won't believe me. Well you tell him we saw him talking to himself in the mirror the day of his wedding to your mother when no one was around, he said wish you were here mom and dad, tell him we heard him and we were standing right beside him.

We love your father, mother and you my dear we have been there every step of the way. The two of them turn slowly and disappears in air. Ionia waives good-bye and turns to walk toward her father and sees him watching her.

As Ionia reaches Ken he asks her about whom she was talking to, so she starts to explain that it was her grandmother and grandfather. Like Ionia figured he didn't believe her so, she told him about the fire and how it happened from what they said and also told him about his wedding day; upon hearing his child say things that he only knew and never talked about he drops the flags he was holding and falls to his knees in tears.

Daddy I didn't mean to make you cry! Oh it's okay sweetheart these are tears of happiness. I believe you now. Ken wipes the tears from his eyes, smiles at his daughter, and picks up the flags from the ground and stands up.

Let's finish putting the rest of these flags on the graves and go home.

With ice cream in hand Ken and Ionia returned home to see Sam still sitting behind the computer just like when they left. Hey Sam we brought you some ice cream. Thank you guys; did you have a good time? Yes we did mommy. Sam, I say let's go to the pool today it's about 80 degrees out and it's a beautiful day! That sounds like a great idea Ken.

Ken, I have to tell you something. Sure Sam. Sam looks over at Ionia. Sweetie go ahead upstairs and get your bathing suit together I will be up there in a minute. Okay mommy! Ionia runs up the stairs and into her room.

I know that we haven't talked about what happened the other night since it happened, but I have done some looking and found something.

Sam pulls out some papers on articles that she had read on the internet about people who had experienced the same thing that she has. It says hear that what the call what happened to me is a succubus.

I have never heard of that before Sam. Me either Ken some people say it's a witch that rides you, it also says that it doesn't happen often but it does; there are cases of people getting hurt while this happens. That is crazy Sam. It says that they are bad spirits that try to steal your soul for another chance to come back.

Well I believe there is a more powerful force that is protecting us and that is God! I have to tell you Sam; I believe Ionia is truly seeing things or people. Why do you say that Ken? Sam she spoke to my parents, she said things that them and I would only know about.

Our daughter is different. Just like she told you about Angie and well how she describes the way that Keyvon died. Sam breaths in deep trying to take it all in because she knows there is truth to what he is saying.

Ionia races down the stairs interrupting their conversation with a smile. Sam let's finish this at another time okay. Okay Ken. The three of them grabs the rest of the things they need for their outing and head out the door to the swim pool.

Chapter 9
Coming To Terms

It's been a week to the day since the Murphy's have come to grips with the fact that their daughter was different from any other child, they haven't had the chance to really sit down and talk about much of anything in the past couple of days.

Between school coming to a close soon in June for Ionia, Sam having to take on a heavier workload at her job and Ken although collecting on his retirement from the military; he decided to take on a part time job to supplement his income.

The Murphy's decided to just take the day and relax together by watching some movies, playing outside with Ionia, and maybe even later they thought they could break out the board games from the closet.

Sam and Ken finish up cleaning the kitchen after having and afternoon lunch, they had made grilled cheese sandwiches because it was Ionia's favorite. Ken decides to wash the dishes while Sam dries and Ionia takes the job of sweeping the floor.

The last pair of dishes and sets of glasses are neatly placed inside the cabinets so Sam reaches over and grabs the dustpan inside on the cleaning closet so she can help Ionia pick up the trash Ionia has swept up in the middle of the floor.

You did a great job Ionia! Thanks mom, I'll dump the trash in the trashcan. Ionia do you want to watch "Finding Nemo" after this? Yes daddy that would be fun.

The three of them leave the kitchen and make their way into the living room. Ionia sits down in her snow-white bean chair after moving it to the center of the room right in front of the television.

Ken goes into the entertainment cabinet to look through the collection of movies to find the right movie. Humph! That's odd! What's wrong Ken? I put the movie right here in between Lion King and Terminator because we hadn't watched it yet but it's not here.

Well, Ionia I'm sorry sweetheart I can't find it right now, is there another movie you want to watch? Umm, not really, can we go outside and play catch? Sure we can, I will go get the gloves and ball Sam. Okay come on Ionia let's get your shoes on and get the bat.

Ken, Sam and Ionia make their way to the backyard and set up the tee stand and ball. Ken and Sam walk further out into the yard and get's ready for Ionia to swing to hit the ball.

Hey batter, batter swing! Ken and Sam chant in the yard. Ionia swings the bat and sends the ball flying past her dad and mom as they try to dive for the ball. Oh, I'm sorry are you hurt? We're okay, that was a good hit though. No not you guys the boy standing over there!

Ken and Sam look into the direction Ionia is standing and sees nothing. Ionia places the bat down and walks over to swing set and stands there. It was a young child who seemed to be about her age he was wearing a baseball cap with the letter "D' on the front with curly black hair peeking out from the sides.

The little boy looks to her and laughs. I'm okay didn't hit me at all; I love baseball though you think that I could play with you sometime? Sure that would be fun. Where do you live and what is your name?

My name is Jessie and my house is right around the corner about 4 doors down; my mom and dad have moved though but it's still my house.

I went to the lake with my parents one summer and I just got so tire, I tried to swim back but it was too hard, so I drowned there. That is so sad to hear, well we can be friends if you like. Great I would like that.

Ionia's attention is pulled away by the sound of tires rolling up the driveway. Grandma, Grandpa! The car comes to a stop as Frank and Francis step out. Hi mom, Hi dad what; what do we owe the pleasure for the visit! Oh we were driving by on our way from the store and decided to see if you were home; Ionia left her little slippers over to the house last weekend so we wanted to drop them off we know that they are her favorite.

Thank you, thank you! Your welcome Ionia. Ken and Sam decide not to tell them about what Ionia was just doing because they were not sure about how they would take it. So you guys out playing a little ball huh? Yeah dad, and I must say she sure can hit the ball.

The four of them continue to have their conversation while Ionia runs off to talk to her friend Jessie. Right out of nowhere in the middle of talking they hear a strange sound coming out of the house.

Sam and Ken had left the windows cracked a little to let the air circulate through the house. They felt this was best so that it would keep the cost of their electric bill down.

Crack! Crack! Smash! Ken grabs the bat from off of the ground and hurriedly walks to the door of the house and opens it slowly. Oh my God! What is it son? You will never believe this.

Frank turns to Sam and Francis. You guys wait here. Frank makes his way to the door cautiously but comes to a complete stop once he reaches the door.

Both Ken and Frank are now standing at the door with mouth drawn open so the two women decide that they want to take look as well so they follow suit.

The kitchen that had once been clean now had food thrown from the cabinets all up against the walls, the refrigerator door was wide open with milk spilling from it, pots and pans wildly set on the stove, glasses shattered everywhere; except for the wine glasses on the counter.

The wine glasses however where not just sitting on the counter the oddest thing they had ever seen in fact, where that these glasses were stacked neatly and perfectly forming the number 3. How in the hell I mean what in the hell is this?

This is impossible this kitchen was spick and span only moments ago and the glasses on the counter that cannot be possible! Ken steps over the food and glass pieces clutching a hold of his bat tighter walking through every nook and cranny of their home.

No one is here guys.   Anger
and confusion has deeply set into
Ken while Sam hurries and grabs
her phone snaps a picture of the
wine glasses. What a mess in
here.

Meanwhile:

Ionia is outside talking to Jessie.
  Hey I told you my name what
is yours? Oh, my name is Ionia. I
have seen you around Ionia; I just
didn't know you could see me.
You have to be careful I have
seen a really bad thing walking
and gliding in and out of your
house.   Yeah I have seen it too
Jessie.

It scares me I don't want it to
hurt anyone.   Ionia it is mad, it
wants you it wants to take over
your soul, you are unique news
travels fast here on this side; you
have a gift that not everyone has.

I just didn't know how true it was until now. Ionia at all cost you must never give in always protects the light inside of you it is from the truest of all higher power.

The dark one did that inside of your house. When you channel to this side be very careful and listen to your gut feelings. Thanks Jessie I will, well I have to go now I will talk to you later.

Ionia waves to her friend and walks towards the house as she sees her grandmother watching her she smiles. Ionia who are you talking to? I was talking to Jessie; he told me that he drowned a couple of years at the lake. Really that is odd Ionia.

Francis looks over to Sam with her eyebrows raised slightly. I remember a couple of years back in the news paper a little boy drowning in the Lake in Holland, poor boy's legs just gave out on him and his family was devastated; I believe they left the neighborhood after that.

Yes that is what he said Grandma he said that he lived just a couple of doors up. Yes dear it was the Thompson's their son's name was Jessie. How could you know that? I told you I was talking to him Grandma. Everyone's face goes blank.

I know one thing this house needs to be blessed as soon as possible there is too much negative energy in here. Sam I know of a Lady that specializes in this type of situation, she is a medium and a hypnosis I will set up an appointment with her for you guys if you like.

Yes mom that would be very helpful if you did and in the mean time if you could speak with the pastor of the church to come and bless the house that would be great as well. The four of them get started on picking up the mess in the kitchen and part their ways after.

Chapter 10
A Surprise Beyond Wildest Dreams

Ding, Dong! Ken opens the door to see Pastor Charles E. Stevens standing at his door ready and willing to help Ken and his family.

Pastor Charles is a tall man who stands about an even 7 feet tall slender in build, wearing all black clothes other than a white square on his collar.

Come in Pastor! Thank you Ken. Have a seat; do you need anything to drink? A glass of water would be good thanks. Sure thing, I hope you don't mind a cup because all of our glasses were shattered. I don't mind at all.

Ken walks into the kitchen to fix an ice cup of water for the Pastor while Sam and Ionia goes into the living room to greet him. Thanks for coming Pastor we really appreciate you being here. Sam and Ionia take a sit on the love seat adjacent from him.

Ken returns from the kitchen with a glass of water and hands it to Pastor Charles. Ken and Sam tell me what is going on. Ken and Sam begin to tell him of all of the happenings from the times since before Keyvon had died all the way up to the present day.

Pastor Charles just sat there listening to all that had accrued without judgment or interruption, and when the two came to the conclusion of their testimony, the pastor took in a deep breath and asked them a series of questions.

Ken and Sam how is your faith with God? The two of them look at each other and then back at him. We try to keep our faith going at all times Pastor, we haven't been to church in a long time it seems but we still carry a love of God with us.

We have had our trying times and we have treaded off the path but we always come back to it. Since our son died it has been truly hard to make it on a day-to-day basis. We also had marital problems just before his passing as well but we know that it has not just been us that keeps us moving.

The pastor opens up a brown leather suitcase that he had brought in with him and pulls out a cross, bible and some holly water. I want you to always remember that you never walk this life alone it is in those times you were being carried through your storms.

At this time I am going to walk through each and every room with prayer from door to door placing holy water at every threshold, I need for you to walk with me each and every one of you so that this can be a united front.

The four of them go through each room and watch as he dabs holy water at each threshold followed with a little prayer. They reach the living room at the end and the pastor and turns around to face Ken and Sam. There is uneasiness here. If you should need me again I'm only a phone call away.

Thank you Pastor will do. Now am I going to see you guys in church on Sunday; we would love to see you there? We will be there Pastor Charles. Ken and Sam watch as Pastor Charles places his bible and holy water vile back into a case and then placing it into the suitcase.

The two of them walk Pastor Charles to the door and watch as he gets in the car and drives off. Ken closes the front door and follows Sam back into the living room and the both sit together on the couch.

Oh, remember we have that appointment with Lidia today for Ionia babe. Ken looks down at his watch to see what time it is. What time was the appointment Sam? I set it for 4 o'clock today. Then that means we have just enough time to get ready and head down there it is already 2 o'clock.

Okay well let's get this going then.
Ionia is sitting on the floor sitting with her legs crossed over and under one another playing with her baseball when Sam and Ken

notice that she is rolling the ball away from her and the ball is rolling back to her on its own.

Ionia baby how are you doing that? I'm playing with Jessie, he says Hi and you almost sat on him earlier.
Sam looks over to Ken with a nervous face. Tell him that I said I'm sorry. Ionia rolls the ball on the floor to Jessie and it comes back to her. He says it's okay he knows that you didn't mean too.

Princess tell Jessie that you will play with him a little later okay, we have to go somewhere. Okay mommy I will. At an instance Ionia's face turns scared. Troy! Troy where are you? Keep it away from me, mommy it's the dark thing!

The dark mass grabs a hold of Ionia's leg and pulls her into the dining room with her parents running after. Jessie stands up and tries to tackle it but his little soul is too weak. Troy appears out of nowhere and grabs the tail of the dark entity and drags it away while fighting it.

Ken picks up his daughter terrified out of his wits at this point while Sam grabs their shoes and keys. Ionia sobbing out of control because nothing like that had happened to her before. They decided that they needed to have an answer now about what is going on in their house and more importantly with their daughter.

After about a 45-minute drive they meet at the house of Lidia Rochester. They had to drive from Grand Rapids to Kalamazoo to a small quaint home off of Alcote Street.

They were not sure of how Francis had come into contact with this lady and they really didn't care they had just hoped that she wasn't a fake just looking for money.

Sam rings the doorbell, and a short blonde haired woman opens the door with a smile; she had looked like she was in her early 40's. Lidia dressed comfortably with jeans and a grey tee shirt that read, "Wouldn't you like to know."

Come in I have been expecting you guys, and who is this beautiful little girl? Hi I'm Ionia! Nice to meet you my dear. You must be Ken and Sam. Yes we are, we are sorry about coming really early I know that we were not suppose to be here until 4:00. Oh, that is okay I had a cancellation anyway.

Have you ever been to a medium and or hypnosis before? No we haven't this is very new to us. Okay I will explain to you how it works; the both of you will be with us when I speak with her. I will put her into a dream like state where she will be able to go back into time and space so we can get to the bottom of things. This will be a painless procedure.

I can tell you guys though just from looking at her she is a very special girl. There is a light that shines around here and many who have passed on surround her, she has been chosen. The road for her will not be easy for her ahead she will be in a battle where good and evil meet and she must prevail, her life will depend on it.

Ionia can you come here please, it's okay. Ionia goes over to Lidia and Lidia in turn has her lay on a couch with a single chair place beside it. Ken and Sam can you have a seat right over there on the couch please?

The two of them take a seat not too far from Ionia. Now it is very crucial that you remain completely silent during this process okay. Yes we will. Ionia I need for you to relax and listen to the sound of my voice okay. Ionia nods her head in agreement.

Lidia reaches over to a table just behind Ionia's head and starts a gadget that sounds like a rhythm of continuous ticks. Ionia you are now drifting into a peaceful sleep where you see multiple colors of a beautiful rainbow, we are now going to travel together back in time to a place long forgotten.

Tell me what do you see child. Ionia starts to recant all that only Ken, Sam and Keyvon would know. She saw the day at his party his preschool friends, Spiderman toys, kisses, hugs, and all conversations that only he had shared but she said as if it where her. Ionia said that she remembered going into a tunnel after going to sleep.

She had even said that her grandparents had met her there in the place called heaven. Ionia stated that she had been able to view her life all though short and was given the chance to come back and make a difference not only in her parent's lives but those around her.

Ionia explains that all though frightened at times she could see people who had passed away and are no longer in the physical world.

Ken and Sam watching from the sidelines begin to cry because they are met with memories of a time passed and that they wish were not cut short, but also confused as to how their little girl could know of things that happened well before her arrival.

After about an hour, which seemed like an eternity had past of questions from Lidia for Ionia she had all that she needed to hear. Ionia when I snap my fingers you will come back to us feeling refreshed as ever; one, two, three. Snap!

Ionia opens her eyes and sits up to see that her mom and dad are crying like newborn babies holding hands. Lidia places her hands on Ionia's back to reassure her that everything is okay. Then she speaks to Ken and Sam in the most sincere way:

Not many are born into this world that posses such extraordinary gift as your daughter has. Ionia is able to see beyond this realm and into the next. You see there is a thin line that separates us from the other side, not only that she has been to heaven and back. There is a darkness that is on a quest for her soul and she will need you to help her see it through.

More importantly as unfounded as it may seem to you, the reason why she has told you of so many things before her time is what many call reincarnation in other words, the same soul returning again for another lifetime; very rare though this soul has traveled back to the same family; So without further adieu Kenny and Sam I'd like to re introduce you to Keyvon.

Melisha Ross

Thanks for reading Ionia; the 3rd release from MELISHA ROSS. We really appreciate your support; please be sure to leave a review and remember to tell a friend. You may also read more titles from *Melisha Ross* and any of the other PRINTHOUSE BOOKS Author's. All titles are available anywhere that books

are sold and reviews can be read
on our website.

It is a theory that women's minds are very complex. This author believes differently. Like their counter the male; women love, they suffer loss, have self-esteem issues, and are always on the path to find what truly makes them happy. My belief is; the only thing that separates the two, are the way they process the same thoughts.

The creator of this book wants to take you on a journey. This journey is filled with love, heartache, finding peace, suffering, loss, acknowledging their beauty, realizing the strength within, and finding true self.

From the backdrop of the ATL; the hottest city in the South, comes a compelling love story about several friends and their adventures in College at the A.U and their professional careers while in the city of Atlanta. Experience Love, Drama, infidelity and historic memories as you indulge yourself in this Romantic tale of fiction. Set in 2001-2002, you're sure to reminisce back when Jay-Z, Nelly, Luda, Missy, 112, Lil Jon, Alicia Keys and more were in heavy rotation on your favorite radio station. When T.I's album; I'm Serious had the city

crazy, the clubs closed late and Ying Yang had those ATL Shake stages rocking and dollars raining.

Everlasting Romance, An American Love Story explores the essence of friendships, life, Love and how those bonds molded several individuals into a close knit family while in the hot city of Atlanta. Donnie, Quentin, Chantel, Cynthia and their friends; found themselves sharing love at every level; Brotherly, Sisterly and most of all intimately! But; at what cost!

Ionia

www.PrintHouseBooks.com
Read it, Enjoy it, Tell a friend!
Atlanta, GA.

All titles available everywhere; that books are sold in the US, Canada, UK, Europe, Australia and New Zealand in Paperback, Hardcover and eBook.

VIP INK Publishing Group, Inc.

PRINTHOUSE BOOKS

Atlanta, GA.